COLD COCKED

By

David Owain Hughes
&
Peter Oliver Wonder

Edited by
Jonathan Edward Ondrashek

A HellBound Books Publishing LLC Book
Houston TX

**A HellBound Books LLC
Publication**

Copyright © 2018 by HellBound Books Publishing LLC
All Rights Reserved

Cover and art design by HellBound Books Publishing LLC

**No part of this book may be reproduced, stored in a retrieval system,
or transmitted by any means, electronic, mechanical, photocopying,
recording or otherwise without written permission from the author
This book is a work of fiction. Names, characters, places and incidents
are entirely fictitious or are used fictitiously and any resemblance to
actual persons, living or dead, events or locales is purely coincidental.**

www.hellboundbookspublishing.com

Printed in the United States of America

Other David Owain Hughes Titles

Novels, Novellas and Short Story Collections:
All-Wound Up
Wind-Up Toy
Wind-Up Toy: Broken Plaything
Wind-Up Toy: Chaos Rising
White Walls and Straitjackets
Escapees and Fevered Minds
Choice Cuts
Walled In
Man-Eating Fucks
Man-Eating Fuckers
The Rack & Cue
Collision Course
Granville
Home Improvements
Psychological Breakdown
Brain Damage
Puckered

Anthologies:
Shadows and Teeth Vol. 3
Trapped Within
Hell of a Guy
Unleashing the Voices
Rejected for Content Vol. 4, 5 & 6
Crossroads in the Dark Vol. 1 & 2
Fifty Shades of Slay
How to Cook a Baby
Madame Movora's Tales of Terror
Big Book of Bootleg Horror Vol. 1, 2 & 3
Shopping List
Depraved Desires
Easter Eggs and Bunny Boilers
Bah! Humbug!
Slashing Through the Snow
VS Vol. 1 & 2
Black Candy
Into the Abyss

Compiled & Edited Anthologies:
What Goes Around
Man Behind the Mask
Fuck the Rules

David Owain Hughes & Peter Oliver Wonder

COLD COCKED

efore arriving by car—the drive taking less than fifty minutes—Betty had been confident. Her plot was solid, her mind unwavering. But now, as she stood before the old wrought-iron gates, which reminded her of something out of Hammer Horror, she felt her best-laid plans unravel inside her screaming mind.

This is a bad idea, she thought, looking up at the metal fence adorned with sharp iron spikes that wrapped the massive yard.

With a Hessian sack containing the tools she would need for her task over one shoulder, and her daddy's 'borrowed' bolt cutters over the other, Betty tried to calm herself with positive thinking.

If all goes wrong or I'm unsuccessful, I don't have to do it again. I'll think of something else.

Putting her sack down by her side, which gave off a muffled *clink -clank,* Betty hefted the bolt cutters off her shoulder and looked at the tool. Its robust cutting jaw sent a shiver down her spine.

I wouldn't want my nips caught in it!

She pulled her gaze from it and settled on the gate, which was held shut by a bulky chain with an impressive padlock clasped to it.

Are we sure this is the best way in? Betty thought. *Maybe there's a gap in the fence? A railing out or bent? No, we did a perimeter check last week. There's no weakness. It's either this way or climb the fence and try to avoid . . .* Her thoughts tapered off as she looked up at the gleaming spikes.

Betty shook her head and stepped to the gates, her pussy twitching as an image flashed across her mind of being impaled through her love tunnel.

With the mouth of the bolt cutters spread wide, she got close to the thick chain, fed it into the tool and snapped it shut with all her might. "Come on," she gasped, heat flushing her face. Sweat dribbled down her forehead and temples. "Come on, come on!" Her hands shook and her thighs trembled—the urge to piss was strong. And then a link snapped and the heavy-duty chain gave way. With a deafening roll of steel, the shackle fell from the entrance and hit the ground with a dense thump.

Betty looked around.

The night was silent.

All she could hear was the beating of her heart and the blood in her ears.

If anyone should catch me . . .

With a delicate push, she opened the gate and waited for the impending scream of unoiled hinges, but it never came.

Small mercies. However, had the weatherman been right, I wouldn't have to worry about making—

The sky filled with the onset of thunder—small flickers of lightning followed with swift timing.

A smile pulled across Betty's face as she placed the bolt cutters into her sack. She entered the graveyard, slinging the strap of the bag over her shoulder and pulling her balaclava down. Before creeping toward the headstones, Betty unclipped her flashlight from off her utility belt and switched it on—it gave off a weak, perfect glow that didn't illuminate the place like a welcome beacon. With its thin beam, she navigated through the concrete maze with relative ease.

This is going to be a game of chances—I should have done my research by looking at the obits in the papers.

A fat crack of thunder parted the dark clouds, allowing yellow-blue sparks of lightning to shoot through, lighting up her immediate area and giving her a serious case of the heebie-jeebies. Her flashlight trembled, and her heartrate kicked up a few dozen notches.

Betty had never liked stormy weather.

"The gods have their machine guns out again!" her father would often tell a prepubescent Betty with a smile splashed across his face.

"How so, Daddy?"

"The thunder is the barrage of bullets and the lightning is the flicker of muzzles."

The thought of God, Jesus and the rest of the boys taking potshots at each other had always given her the shivers, much like it did now.

Stupid man. I wonder if he'd try telling me the same thing nowadays. Me, a woman of science.

She shook her head and set her face in concentration. When a flicker of electricity lit up a tombstone by her side, Betty turned and flashed her light on it. But she couldn't make out the name and dates chiseled into the granite.

Getting closer, she wiped the dust from it and read aloud, "Here lies Frank E. Stein. Date of death: January 1, 1818." Her beam moved to the gravestone opposite. "Here lies Else M. S. Stein. Date of death: 1935."

A gutsy grumble of thunder roared and sparks filled the sky once more.

"The gods are at it again, Betty . . ." she imagined her father saying.

She shivered, scanning the headstones in front of her. *Too old—there'd be nothing left of 'em,* she thought, moving on.

As she crept, Betty stole glances at the huge, looming house toward the bottom of the cemetery. It belonged to the caretaker. The place remained dark—she hadn't gained his unwanted attention.

Stop being soft! Who in the hell is going to hear me in this weather? It's why I picked tonight.

A few rows over from Frank's and Else's resting places, Betty came across a grave that looked as though it had been filled in of recent—the earth didn't look quite right. When she shined her flashlight at the headstone, she noticed a makeshift marker there suggesting a more sophisticated one was on the horizon.

"Percival F. James," she spoke.

Excellent.

Betty put her bag down, opened it and removed a shovel and crowbar in readiness.

Before starting to dig, she gave the storm ten minutes to reach its zenith, feeling it wasn't quite overhead. When the booms and flashes came at a startling pace, Betty slammed the tip of her shovel into the soft earth and dug, flinging loads over her shoulder in a haphazard manner.

When the heat under her balaclava became unbearable, she rolled it up, thinking it safe to do so.

As she continued deeper into the grave—two feet, three feet—her jogging pants and vest became filthy and sweat-soaked. On more than a handful of occasions, Betty stopped to catch her breath and wipe the beads of water gathered at the nape of her neck.

After a patient couple of hours, the tip of the shovel struck something hard—the sweet sound of pay-dirt. She wiped her filthy, sweaty forehead with her forearm and took a deep breath. Given the option, she would have avoided the arduous labor inherent in a grave robbing altogether, but laws made it difficult to come by the recently deceased by any other means.

She tossed the shovel to the surface and reached for the crowbar. Stooping, she brushed the dirt from the coffin's edges to expose its nails. She was momentarily surprised before feeling like a total fool: she had been expecting a casket made from planks of wood like the ones in Wild West movies rather than the finely crafted, dome-topped oak box that rested below her.

"I won't need the crowbar after all!"

She propped herself up on the earthen walls Spiderman-style and lifted the lid of the death-box. The dense, cold fog of heinous smells rose from the decaying pile of bones, putrid meat, and dusty rags. She felt the vapor as it dissipated from the coffin, and sealed her lips to avoid breathing in any of the godawful fumes.

As she glared down at the remains of a stranger, she made a mental note of this very important lesson: corpses do, indeed, have expiration dates. If she was going to find a way to make this work, she was going to have to go for a fresher body.

"Damn it!" Betty made to get out. "I thought for sure this was a fresh grave, what with the shaky marker and how uneven the dirt looked."

Over her laborious grunts, Betty failed to notice the storm's passing. And, as she inched her way out of the grave, the first drops of fat rain started falling.

Before she could reach solid ground, the once-hard mud walls of Mr. James' place of rest became sloppy, and Betty slipped and slid as her hands and feet lost purchase.

"*Fuck*!" she blurted, falling and crashing down on top of the cadaver, sending a jolt through her coccyx and up her spine—the sound of bones splintering filled her ears as she fell forward to relive the pain at the base of her spine. Betty felt the mad scurry of beasties over her body. "Ugh! *Ew*!" When she placed her hands flat against the corpse's chest to push herself up, it caved in, and she fell back against the body, taking in a lungful of stale dust, her nostrils filling with watery mud that showered down around her.

Soon, she was ankle-deep in water as thick as soup— her trainers clogged.

"Got to get out!"

She rose, making the mistake of looking at the face she was directly above. Slice marks split the flesh that remained, and it looked like the head had probably been decapitated, as there were stitches around the throat.

Betty jumped at a wall and dug her fingers and covered toes deep into it. As she climbed, she growled. Her arms and legs quivered.

Reaching the top, Betty crawled along the ground until she was clear of the grave.

"Fuck, fuck, fuck," she panted, rolling onto her back and pushing herself farther away with the use of her feet, hands, and ass. "Too close a call." Her teeth chattered; her skin prickled.

"Who the fuck's out there?!" someone screamed in the distance.

Betty's head turned in the direction from which she thought she'd heard the voice.

Lights in the caretaker's home burst to life.

"I'll fill ya full of buck, bastard kids." A hound started barking. "Sick 'em, boy! Me and Jessie here gonna teach you to respect the dead."

Betty sprang to her feet, gathered her tools, bag, and flashlight, and ran for the gate.

Something made a piercing snapping sound, which tore the night apart.

His shotgun, she thought, smashing against the cemetery's entrance.

The dog's bark sounded much too close. She heard its tongue flapping wild in its crazed bloodlust—its saliva probably plastering its enormous muzzle.

Satan's hounds of Hell!

Not thinking clearly, Betty pushed the gate instead of pulling and, in the process, rebounded off it and onto her ass.

"Show yourself!" the old man roared. "Come on."

Betty looked over her shoulder and saw a bright light swinging her way.

Scrambling to her feet, she yanked the gate open and raced through it, jumping into her car and fleeing into the night, sobbing. Her breath hitched in her throat, her soggy shoes squelched as she worked the pedals, and her tools jangled on the passenger seat as she drove at a breakneck speed.

***

When she reached her stately home (which was concealed in a gated neighborhood filled with long driveways and fancy cars, and—perhaps best of all—lacking any too-near snooping neighbors), Betty was still sobbing. Once parked, she got out and ran across the graveled drive, kicking up stones, and rushed inside her house. With the front door closed, she slumped against it and slid down the wood into a crumpled heap. She bawled like a three-year-old in mid-tantrum. Her cheeks flushed. Betty slammed her fist against a wall, yelled and pulled her hair.

"Stupid! Stupid, stupid, *stupid*!" she chanted.

Betty cracked herself across her face with the flat of her palm, provoking fresh wails and more tears. Pulling her knees up, she buried her face between her thighs. Her body trembled, and snot shot out of her nostrils. "I—I—could have been *killed*!" Her breath hitched. "And for what? Science?! I'm too young to die!"

But think of the fame your creation will bring, Betty—maybe an Albert Einstein World Award of Science? A Wolf Foundation Prize? A Nobel Prize? A baby?!

Her tears came to an instant end, and so she wiped her eyes with the back of her hand. When she snorted, strings of mucus vacuumed back up her clogged nostrils. "Yes, a baby . . ." she muttered, nodding as she caught her breath. "I need to pull myself together."

Betty straightened, placed the back of her head on the door and stared into the darkness that filled the room. She found it calming as she took in slow, controlled breaths and blew them out her mouth. She listened to the whoosh of each exhale, trying to relax her internals. When her emotions were under wraps, she pushed herself off the floor, walked the length of the hallway— her feet squelching—to where the light switch was and flicked it. Brightness filled the space, and when Betty turned, she found thick, muddy footprints on the wooden floor and mucky handprints on the walls here and there.

She shrugged. "Easily remedied."

Before setting off for the living room, Betty removed her sneakers, clothes, and underthings. With everything balled under her arm, she moved through the house, turning on lights as she went. After she reached the kitchen and threw everything into the washing machine, Betty filled a bucket with warm, soapy water and took it back to the hallway, where she scrubbed the floor and walls.

Finished cleaning, she made her way upstairs to her bedroom, grabbed a fresh towel off the radiator, and headed to her on-suite for a shower. She desperately needed to scrub the smell of death, failure, and the night's horrible memories away.

While the shower ran, Betty looked in the mirror and brushed her hair through to remove the knots before washing it. Like her shoes, it too was filled with mud, along with slime, leaves, and bone fragments. She even found a couple of worms writhing in it. The treasures fell and gathered in the sink.

"*Ew!*"

Betty turned the taps on and washed the mess down the plughole. A shiver snaked down her back.

"You look like hell, Betty," she told her reflection. Small bruises had gathered across her forehead, and there were gashes on her cheeks and chin—one eye was slightly puffy and colored purple-yellow. Her body sported nicks and cuts. Her left elbow was skinned.

"Disgusting."

Betty turned from the mirror, unable to look at herself—not because of the damage, but rather because of the image of the fat woman with one tit bigger than the other that she saw beneath her reflection. The 'obese bitch' the men loved to tease. Even though she'd lost most of the weight years ago and had had a boob job to correct her breasts, Betty couldn't move past it.

Don't think about it! she thought, stepping under the hot spray. The water sluiced the filth, leaves, bits of twigs, and other lumps of shrapnel she'd picked up from the cold grave, including more beasties that had gathered in her thick pubic hair.

"Get out, you vile things!" she screamed, scrubbing her pussy with a lathered sponge. "Ugh." Betty pulled pained expressions as she stepped on and squished the bugs, their guts pushing between her toes. Her stomach flipped and her throat filled with spew, but she gulped it down and aimed her feet under the rays of water, washing the obliterated creatures towards the drain on fluffy pads of suds.

The plughole began to block with the debris, and so Betty bent over and cleared it with a finger before she found herself once again ankle-deep in brown-colored water.

She shivered at the memory.

What if the old man had come along and filled the hole in with me inside instead of shooting or turning me over to the police? I could have been buried alive! Stuck to die with that horribly disfigured corpse . . .

"Don't be foolish," she said.

A cold feeling crept down her spine. Her insides shriveled.

Betty pushed the thoughts from her mind and concentrated on soaping her voluptuous body—a body she'd worked hard to achieve—and enjoyed it, now that it was clean and gleaming. She moaned when she grabbed her surgically enhanced tits and molded them, the nipples standing firm. With one hand, Betty removed the showerhead from off the bracket affixed to the wall and pressed it against her cunt, the spray seeking out her g-spot—without a man to satisfy her, she had to do it herself.

"*Ooh!*"

Betty's cheeks reddened as she slipped a finger behind and inserted it into her anus with care and precision.

She gasped—an explosion went off inside her guts, head, and pussy. Dizziness contorted her vision, and then, in the distance, she caught the sound of shrill ringing.

"Ignore it," she told herself, but the noise kept coming, irritating her and breaking her concentration. "Fuck." Betty slammed her fist against the wall at her side and replaced the showerhead.

Only one person would ring me this early, and if I don't answer, she'll give me hell for days, she thought, turning the taps off.

She rushed out of the shower, wrapped her robe around her naked, wet body and crossed to her phone. The vibrations against the marble countertop rang out through the large bathroom; the glass and solid surfaces amplified the sound. The ringtone *was* that of her mother's, confirming what she already knew.

"Mother, I wasn't expecting a call from you," she said, trying to make her smile apparent through the cell.

"Betty, a thought just crossed my mind," she said dryly. "It's been awhile now since you last tried on the dress for your sister's wedding. I was worried you may have put on a few pounds since then and want to make sure you look decent for such a special occasion . . . We wouldn't want a repeat of what happened in the bridal shop, now would we?!"

Every muscle in her body contracted as the memories and shame from *that* day two years ago flooded her brain, making Betty snap her teeth together and grind them to stop herself from yelling.

You swore—swore!—we'd never speak of, or even mention, *that moment ever again, Mommy . . .*

***

That afternoon at the Blushing Bride wedding shop had been a long, hot, sticky, and testing one for Betty and her mother. Mother, who made Betty try on a dozen or so dresses, came up with reasons for not liking the clothes that ranged from absurd to rude: "The colors are wrong, the design isn't right for a lady of your . . . er . . . size, I don't like it, it has silly flowers on it, there's something funny-looking about the tag, it's too short, it's too long . . ."

She was inexhaustible.

By this point, her poor father had slumped into a chair, boredom etched across his face as he fanned his drenched brow.

"Why couldn't your sister have made you a bridesmaid, hmm? Then we wouldn't have all this aggravation, would we? If only you tried to get along with Veronica, Bet—"

"I'll try harder in the future, Mom," Betty cut her off, fearing she was about to fly off the handle and stab her mother's eyes out with the heel of a stiletto. "Promise."

"I do hope so."

Betty tuned out, her eyes latching onto a ruby-colored dress with a plunging neckline and revealing slit up one side. It was to die for.

I have to have it! she thought, pushing past her mother and snatching it from the rack.

Size 14, the label read.

"That won't fit!" Diane grabbed the rag from her daughter's hands and was about to put it back on the rail.

"It will, Mother—I'm down to a size 12 these days."

"Huh! Don't kid yourself, dear," she said, eyeing her daughter up and down.

"Well, we'll just see about that, won't we?" Betty took the dress and stormed off toward the changing room.

Ten minutes later, with the garment about containing her, Betty stepped from the changing room clutching her stomach.

"See, I told you, Mother."

"Care to breathe, dear?" she replied with an acid look.

Don't like it, do you? Betty smiled inwardly. *Don't like the fact that I'm right and you're wrong, and that I'm slim and att—*

Betty's victory was short-lived, and before she could wish she'd left her bra on underneath the gorgeous piece of clothing, seams ripped. The zipper blew off, catching her mother in the cheek, tearing a gash that beaded red.

"Oh, God!" her father yelled, seeing the dress slip down his daughter's body.

In that split second, her worst nightmare was lived: Betty's misshapen tits, one breast being two cup sizes bigger than the other, were on display for her parents to see; so too were her stretch marks.

Someone nearby laughed.

Another person gasped.

Betty turned, crying, and fled for the changing rooms.

After Betty was coaxed out of her hiding place by her parents, the shop assistant, and owner, she was frog-marched out of the place to another where she hadn't had a say in what she would be wearing. It took her mother less than ten minutes to find the most godawful rag she could, pay for it, and leave.

Betty, who remained silent, hadn't been able to look at her parents, her dad especially.

That night, the dreaded question came in the safety of her bedroom, away from her father. "Why didn't you tell me about . . ." Diane had pointed at Betty's cleavage.

"Oh God, Mom!"

"Well, they look bloody terrible—wonky, mismatched ski slopes, that's what they are. No man will ever want . . ." She trailed off. "Thank Christ this day is over. I've never been so humiliated, Betty. I don't want you talking about this with anyone, do you hear me? We certainly won't be speaking of it ever again."

Tell anyone? she wanted to scream and rip at her mother's face with her nails. *Are you fucking crazy?!*

***

"Betty, are you daydreaming?"

"Er, yeah, sorry," she said. Though her jaw was clenched, she forced a laugh. "Actually, I just finished a rather rigorous workout, and I was in the shower when you called. Perfect time to try the dress again. You're always right, of course."

"I'd just hate for anything to ruin such a special occasion. Also, it probably wouldn't hurt to do a few more gym sessions before the big day gets here. Don't neglect the cardio. Now is the time to set good habits, dear. If you try hard enough, you might be able to find yourself a good man at the event, especially now you've had your *girls* corrected."

Betty let out another fake laugh. "Okay, Mom. I'll keep that in m—"

The sound of a dial tone was as good a goodbye as she could expect from that dreadful woman. She never had been big on ending conversations on a high note, at least not for as long as Betty could remember.

Bitch. Bringing up my weight and men. You always were vindictive . . .

Up until the moment of her birth, her parents had been under the impression they were having a boy. They were intensely disappointed at the doctor's announcement when Brian came out without a penis. Just before they'd conceived, they'd received news that Diane had cervical cancer and would need a hysterectomy as soon as possible before it spread.

They'd been crushed by the knowledge that they would never have the lad they wanted, and they'd taken their disappointment out on her ever since. At least, her mother had, inadvertently leading Betty to become the single woman she seemed to despise today.

When in school, Betty had been driven to eat her feelings of self-loathing away and became quite large by the time she discovered boys and was the victim of severe and near constant bullying. It had been so bad that she took a year off between high school and college to dedicate her life to getting in shape and learning about nutrition. By the time she was sitting in her first freshman class, she was one of the most beautiful women on campus.

However, where men were concerned, she'd led a lonely life, and had found it impossible to be intimate with a man since her last time, which had also been her first.

***

Troy was the first person to make her feel like she was a beautiful woman. They had met in medical school as part of a study group. He'd held revision sessions at his apartment to learn about fetal development.

One night, as per usual, drinks were offered as they read and took notes. When it was time for everyone to depart, he held Betty back.

"Whoa, there," he said as she stumbled through the door.

His hand cuffed around her forearm. Butterflies exploded in her gut. Her panties soaked through.

"Is something the matter?" she asked, looking him up and down.

Ignoring the final goodbye from another group member, Troy said, "I think, just maybe, you've had a little too much to drink to drive home." His dazzling white smile brought a tremble to her knees.

"Is that so?" she asked, staggering forward and placing a hand on his firm chest.

He nodded.

"Well, what should we do about that?"

"I could give you a ride home," he suggested. A loud crack came from somewhere in the distance.

"Was that a gunshot?" Betty asked, looking out into the parking lot of the apartment complex.

"Uh, it was probably a car backfiring."

"Whatever it was, I don't want to leave my car here or anywhere else I'm not staying, that's for sure. My parents just bought it for me and they would absolutely kill me if anything happened to it."

"I see. In that case, you've left us with two options: either I drive your car to your place, in which case I'd have to walk home, or you and your car stay here with me."

"And what would we do if I *did* stay here?"

Troy stroked the exposed skin on her arm as he shut the front door with the other hand. "Well, we could keep studying, if you'd like."

Betty walked to the couch and fell backwards onto it. A shocked look overcame her face. "Cold, *cold, cold*!" she said, sitting bolt upright.

"Oh, shit," Troy said, retrieving a towel from a hall closet. "I'm sorry. I think Dale must have spilled his beer earlier." He wrapped the cloth around her and pulled her face close to his chest, squeezing the rag against her back. "God, that asshole must have fallen asleep and tipped his whole damn drink. Fucking lightweight," he said, laughing.

Betty's heart melted. This was a closeness she'd never allowed herself to experience in the past. Her nipples stood erect and her clitoris throbbed beneath her short skirt. She lifted her heels off the floor, standing on her tiptoes to kiss him. She opened her mouth and allowed his tongue to slide in. She pulled away slowly and gazed at him in awe.

"So, I've got some bad news." Troy held a deadpan countenance.

Betty's heart sank. She did her best to keep the horrified expression to herself.

"I was going to sleep on the couch tonight, but since it's soaked in beer, I think we're going to have to share my little bed. I hope you don't mind getting close and cuddly."

The serious look on his face evaporated, replaced by a smug grin. She reached up and playfully licked his lips before pushing him back toward the hallway. She followed him step for step until he turned and ran from her. Donning the towel like a cape, she gave chase.

In the box-sized bedroom, Troy fell onto the bed. "Ah, where are my manners?" he asked. "Obviously, we can't have you sleeping in those beer-soaked clothes! Here, let me get you a shirt you can sleep in." He sprang up and made for the closet. From a hanger, he pulled a T-shirt with the logo of a local band. "An extra-large was the last one they had. It's unfortunate that I don't get to wear it out much, but it should be pretty good for you to snooze in."

She took it from him, bringing her face within inches of his before turning. "Excuse me while I go change into something more . . . *comfortable*," she said with a wink, heading into the hall. The bathroom was the first door on the left, she knew from previous study sessions.

Watching herself in the mirror, she unbuttoned her blouse. Every time she saw her reflection, she was flabbergasted. She thought, *Damn, that girl is sexy!* The fat girl was a foggy memory.

Her self-consciousness was once again realized as soon as she pulled the wet shirt from her body. In her youth, she'd cut her flesh in random places as punishment for feeling so worthless. Her stretch marks caught her eye next, and she dreaded what was soon to happen.

But maybe not everyone was as awful as she'd led herself to believe. Troy was sweet. She thought he would understand. *You're not going to be a virgin forever!*

She removed her bra and made certain not to look in the mirror before stuffing her head into the shirt and covering herself once more. Next, she removed her skirt, folded up all her clothes, and placed them on the counter. She lifted the neck of the shirt to her nose and inhaled deeply. It smelled like Troy.

Back in the right frame of mind, she exited the bathroom and returned to the bedroom. Troy was lying on his stomach, his nose in a book. She rested her arm against the doorframe and arched her back, striking a sexy pose. "I'm not interrupting, am I?"

He rolled over. His eyes widened as he looked from the book to her nice, smooth, bare legs. "Not quite yet, but you're welcome to try harder." The right corner of his mouth rose.

Betty ran to him, pressing her mouth against his. She slid her tongue between his lips and wrapped her legs around him, pushing him back down on the bed. She sat up and placed her hands on his chest, feeling his muscles flex. His cock stiffened and pressed against her thighs.

She grinded against it as she leaned in to kiss him. She loved the feeling of his fingers grasping her ass. She pressed her hot opening against his erection, feeling it fill the gap between her pussy lips through his thin pants and her panties.

Betty pulled her mouth from his and slid toward his dick. She pulled his pants down and off. She giggled, looking upon the tent created in his white boxer shorts. Her hands caressed his legs as she made her way back up. She hooked her fingers into the waistband of his underwear and inched them down to reveal his rock-hard prick.

Guided by instinct, she kissed the base, taking the shaft in her hand and massaging it. His groans turned her on further. She opened her mouth and took the tip of his cock in, for the first time in her life getting a taste of pre-come. She worked her mouth up and down as she rubbed his testicles.

"Oh, holy shit—that's incredible." Troy moaned as he placed his hand on the back of her head to guide her. She took him down her throat as far as she could before pulling back to gasp for breath—strands of thick, stringy drool trailed from her lips to his engorged dick.

She pulled his boxers off and sat on him, their genitals separated by nothing more than her soaked panties.

"I want to see your tits," he said.

Without thinking, she grabbed the bottom of the band shirt and pulled it up over her head. The moment the black material passed through her field of vision, she found the expression on Troy's face had changed into a picture of pity. She felt his hardness between her legs shrivel and drain of life.

She followed his gaze to find that he was staring, agog, at the scars along her body.

"Oh," she gasped, pulling the shirt back on. The enormous pain in her chest spread throughout her body like cancer moving at the speed of light. Tears filled her eyes.

She swung her leg over him and climbed out of bed. "I'm so sorry. I thought—"

"No, *I'm* sorry," said Troy, sitting up, reaching for his boxers and putting them on in a hurry. "I just . . . I didn't know . . ."

"Didn't know *what*? That I'm horrible to look at naked? I was so stupid to think anyone could have seen anything different!"

Troy was frozen to the spot.

Vomit rushed out of him with intense velocity.

The world was a blurry mess through her tears but she managed to get her clothes on, find her purse, and make it out to her car without so much as another word from Troy.

She'd fallen for him harder than she had ever thought possible, only for him to see the body she had worked tirelessly on and to be repulsed by the self-inflicted scars of a traumatized young lady. Scars that her mother hadn't even mentioned on *that* day . . . . Horrific though they were, that stupid bitch only saw the very surface of Betty—the tip of the blade had gone far deeper than that awful woman could ever see.

She had been nervous enough taking her shirt off in front of a boy for the first time, but she'd thought he was a sweet guy. They had gotten to know each other and had talked of problems she had assumed they both shared. The look of complete revulsion was something she never wanted to experience again, and she'd learned an integral lesson: the very sight of her naked body was enough to make a horny college kid vomit.

She would have to make it through life without ever knowing the touch of a man again.

A *living* man, anyway.

***

Knocking on death's door hadn't always been a hobby of hers.

Betty's parents were successful scientists: her father, an electrical engineer; her mother, an astrophysicist. Though she'd been unable to earn their affection from birth, they gave her and her sister every opportunity to excel mentally and, when she'd grown, Betty decided to get into the field of medicine. Her original intent had been to become an obstetrician, but she found her sights set on the area of fertility.

First, to appeal to a positive status with her parents, she took the year off after high school to better herself. With her weight under control, she headed off to college and turned her attention to devouring the information in every course she took, always asking for more. After learning all there was to know on the subject of in vitro fertilization, she began her own research. She'd heard the story of a colleague's patient who lost her husband to a fatal car crash before receiving the news that his sample had been damaged due to a faulty seal. Betty thought she'd be able to extract a specimen despite his condition of being less than alive.

After consulting with the morgue, Betty grabbed her medical bag and made the trip to the hospital. The mortician was happy to oblige in her quest to extract living sperm from a dead body, grinning from ear to ear as he slid the slab from behind one of the many small, steel doors on the wall—the cold, blueish cadaver with several injuries jiggled to a halt with the rest of the table. Almost giddily, the mortician watched from over Betty's shoulder for the duration of the procedure.

From within her kit, she removed a syringe, its barrel filled with a milky green serum. After discarding the sheathe from the needle, she injected it into the cadaver's pubis. With both hands, she massaged the serum into the base of his penis. "This ought to enter the vas deferens and into the testis to activate the process that leads to sperm creation."

A sour look crossed the grey-haired man's face. "Madame, is that entirely necessary?"

Giving him the stink-eye, she replied, "It's not exactly like I can rely on the heart to pump the serum trough his system, now can I?" She wrapped her fingers around the lump of flesh resting upon his thighs and began to knead it. It was something she had never done to a man before. Blood rushed to her cheeks. She felt warm all over, aware of herself becoming aroused.

"I've been in this line of work for nearly three decades, and this is the first time I've ever envied anyone on my slab."

"Oh my God." Betty snapped back to reality. Her focus fled the scientific realm and found itself ignoring anything but the mound of flesh in her hand. "Doctor Goodwin, I must insist you either silence yourself or find your way outside. A little bit of professionalism goes a long way and this is a very sensitive procedure that could one day help millions!"

The look on his face morphed into one of shame, his chin dropping. "I apologize, it's just that I—"

"I don't want to hear it," she said, turning back to her work at hand. She realized she still held a firm grip on the penis. When she released it, her handprint remained in the dead tissue.

She pulled another syringe from her bag, this one empty.

"You might want to look away for this part," she said as she inserted the needle into the corpse's right testicle.

Despite her best efforts, that first attempt was a failure. Betty, however, refused to let that serve as a deterrent. Instead, she learned from her findings and continued to explore the field of necrotic semen rejuvenation (NSR). Her peers were fascinated by the possibilities and implications of her research and encouraged her to dig deeper, but with animal testing. And so, she did.

At her office, she performed experiments with rats and monkeys and had several papers published. NSR was her ticket to the top of her field, but still, she did not receive love and respect from her parents. That left her with only one option.

After her incident with Troy, she'd had no desire to attempt to mate with someone who would only wind up hurting her. She'd made up her mind that there was no soulmate out there for her and she would never find true love. She would commit her life to her work instead and planned on succeeding in human trials when she found the perfect father for a child.

She would find the ideal corpse to sire her son. A baby boy for her parents to be proud of.

Finally, she would have the key to her parents' warm embrace.

***

A few nights after her disastrous attempt at plucking a fresh body from a boneyard of her choice, Betty was determined to make amends. In the time between her flop and next attempt, she thought out a fresh plan of attack. This time, she kept her eye on the obits and filled herself with as much confidence as possible before taking another strike at digging up a usable corpse.

"You can't make an omelet without breaking eggs—any chef will tell you that!" she said aloud while studying her work one evening. "Without failure, success doesn't exist, Betty, dear girl."

This time, I'll set out earlier. Going before dawn last time was a mistake.

At one point in her scheming, she thought about breaking into the caretaker's home, drugging his dog, and gagging and tying the old man to his bed. However, the idea of being caught graverobbing was bad enough, without adding breaking and entering and whatever other charges silencing an ancient codger and disabling his mutt would bring to the list.

No, that will never do.

Betty then thought about going to a different graveyard. After all, there were plenty in the small towns and hamlets beyond her city, but the proposal of shifting a stiff seventy to a hundred miles back to her home was off-putting, especially when she had her very own 'meat market' less than fifteen miles away.

"And imagine the stench such a journey would produce!"

No, close by was how it had to be played.

Maybe I could scale the fence or remove a railing or two? Why break the chain? If I keep doing that, they're going to know it's the same culprit—a developed pattern . . . They'll need to catch me first though, I suppose.

She shook her head at that notion. She needed the gates open to get a body out of there. *Besides, I can't very well throw a carcass over the railings, can I? I'm not Fatima Whitbread! But what If I manage to make a gap in the fence?*

Again, she shook her head. Too risky. The gate being open was the only choice.

Anyway, there won't be a third, fourth or fifth effort, because I'll nail it this time around.

But, deep down, Betty wasn't stupid or gullible enough to think she could crack this project on a solid first go—there was no telling if her juice would work. Tweaks may be needed.

It doesn't matter. If I have to rob a body time and again, I'll do it, even if it means going back to the same vine to pluck my grape.

And then her eyes fell on the bolt cutters and she knew exactly what had to be done.

Standing before the haunting cemetery gates once again, her earlier suspicions were confirmed: a new, thicker chain with a reinforced padlock had been secured to the entrance. Still, Betty felt confident as she snapped the tool's jaws open and closed.

"I hope he's taken out shares with Yale!"

Betty placed the cutter over the chains and used it to bite through a link until it cracked and gave way. The heavy-duty restraint fell to the ground. With the gate open, she picked up her bag of tools, unclasped her flashlight, removed a list of the recently deceased from her bra and jogged into the graveyard.

Betty opened the paper and looked at the three names on it: D. O. Hughes, Robert Bernadette, and Mike Chambers. She had little hope of finding any of them, but she felt good in having a guide this time—the three men had been buried within the last twenty to forty-eight hours.

If I can find them, she thought, *I might just get somewhere.*

But seeking them out among the hundreds of graves would be a chore. Still, it gave her something to work off, and she had hours to kill before dawn started breaking.

"I think I'll begin at the front and work my way to the back," she said aloud, walking with speed.

The first row of headstones started within feet of the caretaker's home, but she tried not to think about it, and kept her flashlight beam muffled with a piece of cloth she'd brought with her.

After two hours of lumbering up and down lines of tombstones, struggling to read names and dates with a depleted light, Betty was about ready to pick any grave and start digging, feeling she was coming no closer to finding any of the names on her inventory.

"This is a waste of . . ."

Her words trailed off when her beam fell on a headstone—the grave looked fresh—and she read the name: D. O. Hughes. Betty consulted her list, a smile pulling across her chops.

"*Bingo*!"

She set her things down, opened her bag, removed the spade, and stabbed it into the soft, pliable earth. She worked with speed, stopping only now and then to wipe the sweat from around her eyes, mouth, and brow. In what seemed like record time, Betty was soon scraping the shovel against the casket where one D. O. Hughes rested.

Spiders scampered in her guts. She had the sudden urge to piss.

Throwing the tool up to level ground, she clapped her hands together and hopped up and down on the sarcophagus like an excited child in that proverbial shop.

This is it, Betty! she thought, grabbing the upper part of the coffin and opening it.

"Jesus Christ!" she blurted, jumping back and losing her footing. Betty's head connected with the solid dirt wall at her back. Black spots danced before her. "*Ugh*."

She pushed off the wall, shook her head, and argued with herself that what she'd seen was a mistake, a trick of light. Grabbing her flashlight, she approached the open lid with caution and shined the beam onto the body's face.

Her breath hitched. A gasp escaped her.

D. O. Hughes' mouth was set into a grin, his eyes wide open.

"What the . . ."

She also noticed he was bare-chested.

"I need—"

Betty stopped talking, turned, and lifted the bottom half of the casket. What she saw almost made her fall: the lower portion of the man's body was nude, his cock standing hard and firm.

Had the situation been a different one, Betty would have laughed until she wet herself, but she found the whole thing unnerving.

On closer inspection, she noticed a note attached to the cadaver's inner thigh. With the light on it, Betty read what was written there: "Dear Big Man, I've come to heaven with a hard-on so I can fuck your angels here in the sky. This, in turn, will show you my appreciation for womankind."

Betty's face scrunched; her lips pulled back over her teeth, exposing gums. "What a vile, sexist . . ." she started, looking down at the man's erection. "Well, for your sake, I hope the angels don't judge!"

She then swept the beam of light back to the man's face and looked closely at his mouth. It had been wired into position, and she guessed some of the same trickery had been done to get his cock to stand on end, meaning he might be useless as a test subject.

Betty didn't have time to waste and couldn't take the risk.

"Well, this is a dead end—literally. *Fuck!* Who in the hell would have thought it? If they've done that to his cock, God knows what damage they've done to his reproductive system."

After filling the grave back in without closing the guy's coffin, Betty looked at the headstone once more:

Here lies renowned, slightly eccentric, multi-millionaire horror author D. O. Hughes, aka David Bartholomew Foxtrot Owain Hughes, father to hundreds, husband to countless and word-slinger to multiple tales of terror. Peace out, baby! PS: Nice legs!

"*Slightly* eccentric?!" Betty exclaimed, kicking the stone. "How come I didn't spot all that crap before I started digging?" (A few days later, Betty would learn that D. O. Hughes had died lonely and penniless, and that the engraving on his tomb and the way in which he'd been buried had been in his last will and testament. Upon discovering that, she'd felt bad about how she'd covered him over.)

Picking her tools back up, Betty was about to head up the row of headstones when the next grave over caught her eye, and, for the second time that evening, she was flabbergasted.

"Miranda Berkins," she read.

"*How's 'em tits, Wetty Betty?!*"

The memory of the harsh nickname brought heat to her cheeks.

"Miranda Berkins," Betty said again, the name tasting ugly and sharp inside her mouth. "You and your posse were as cruel as you were clever with your words of hate. 'Wetty Betty', 'Bubble Boob', 'Betty Bitter Snatch', 'Betty Blob' . . . The names were endless, but 'Wetty Betty' was your bitches' favorite."

Betty had heard about Miranda's death. The high school cheerleading bully had been involved in a car smash with her fiancé—a jock, Dean something-or-other, who was three years older and played pro football for the local team The Pirates. He'd been driving drunk, and plowed their car into a wall, killing them outright.

From off the grapevine, Betty had heard all the grotesque little details, which had brought a smile to her face.

"I heard they were picking glass out of her face at the morgue for ten hours!" one girl had stated.

"Not so pretty anymore!" added another.

"Dean's guts were smashed through his back by the engine!" a third girl chirped.

"I heard he was scraped off the hood, and when they pulled his face off, his skin came away like strands of chewing gum!" a man had said, causing them all to laugh.

Betty remembered now—while standing over the grave with hate in her eyes, her nostrils flaring, her grip tightening on her tool bag—the conversation taking place in college, but how those people had known of Miranda escaped her.

They must have known Dean—he was, after all, a superstar.

"I was told Miranda was pregnant, but the baby wasn't Dean's!" someone else had said.

"I heard that too," the first girl confirmed. "The baby lived!"

"I would've loved to have seen her smug face cut to ribbons!" the third girl affirmed.

The others gasped at this, but giggled anyway.

So would I, Betty had thought at the time.

"*Yes*! So. Would. I!" she said in the here and now, removing her shovel and starting to dig like a woman possessed. Betty no longer cared if she should find one of the two remaining bodies she'd come looking for. "I always swore I'd piss on your grave when you were dead—I just didn't think I'd ever get the chance."

As she made her hole, sweating bullets, Betty rambled to herself.

"Made my life hell, whore! For years. You're going to get yours. Maybe I'll cut one of your tits off, see how you like it? Perhaps I'll take you home and lock you in my lab. Keep you there and use you for various experiments."

Betty continued in this fashion until her spade hit wood.

"*Ha*!" she screamed, sounding demented.

Her fingers couldn't work quick enough to open the three-year-old coffin.

"You hated me from kindergarten. That's when the nickname started. You kept at me, didn't you?!"

When the lid opened, Betty clapped sight of the decomposing body of her ex-bully. She gagged, but her stomach settled. The stench was almost unbearable—a green cloud enveloped her. Betty couldn't look away.

And then she was back there, in "little school" as her mother used to call it, with Miranda and her spiteful tribe.

***

"Settle down, children," Mrs. Dobbs hollered. "I understand you're excited about your first day back after summer, but let's try and have a little order, yes?"

Betty liked Mrs. Dobbs, who she thought had a motherly way about her—her face was kind, serene, soft. When she was mad, she didn't look it, and would rarely raise her voice in anger. "We must try harder" was her motto if you'd done something wrong.

"What a flake!" Betty heard Miranda Berkins say to her two friends, Ursula Farming and Rhea Cumming, who laughed without trying to hide it.

"Something funny, girls?" Mrs. Dobbs asked.

"No, Miss," the trio answered.

"Okay." The teacher went on, addressing the class.

"Dozy Dobbs!" Ursula whispered, which was loud enough for Betty to hear.

Betty rolled her eyes and scoffed. "So juvenile," she said, not meaning to say it aloud. She covered her mouth with her hands, but it was too late. She turned to the girls, heat coloring her cheeks.

"What did you say, smart mouth?" Rhea asked. "She's lipping us, girls."

"Going to fatten your lip after school!" Ursula threatened, cracking her knuckles.

"Fucking uppity bitch," Miranda said, looking Betty dead in the eye. "Always thought you were special, didn't you?"

"Are you cursing, ladies?" Mrs. Dobbs asked.

Betty's mouth again betrayed her. "Yes, *they* are, Miss."

"Is that true, Miranda Berkins? You can see me after class."

"But—"

"*After* class," Mrs. Dobbs repeated.

"You're fucking dead meat, Betty," Miranda whispered.

"Going to mess up your piggish face," Rhea piped in.

"I'm sorry, I didn't mean to . . ." Betty started crying. Her legs shook, and then, just like her uncontrollable mouth, she lost power of her bladder. Her urine splashed against the floor, silencing the whole room. "Oh, God. I can't stop!"

"Ha-ha-ha!" a chorus of cackles burst from her side.

"Wetty Betty!" Miranda blurted.

And then the whole class joined in, except for Mrs. Dobbs, of course, who tried her best to settle the children.

***

The laugher from the past brought Betty out of her dream-like state, her eyes refocusing on the body before her. She watched, fascinated, as rats, beetles, worms, maggots and other beasties wormed, snaked, scurried, and moved about the body, poured out of the mouth, empty eye sockets, and ears, and made what little skin was left pulsate as they burrowed beneath it. She could hear the bugs feasting—old, saggy flesh was torn from the once firm, tight, and warm body.

"How's 'em tits, Maggot Miranda?" she asked, looking at the hollowed-out chest with ribs exposed beneath rags. "What's that? I can't hear you."

Her laugh was cold and bitter.

"Well, I'd love to stay and chat, but I have a stud to pick up."

Before getting out of the hole, Betty slipped her yoga pants and thong down her legs, squatted to hover above the remains of Miranda's face and pushed a shit and piss out. The sound of her waste splattering the corpse gave her extreme pleasure, bringing her to the brink of climax.

When she was finished, she turned and looked down at what she'd done. Another laugh escaped her, and she grabbed the shovel and rammed it through the brittle spinal column, separating the head from the rest of the skeleton.

"I hope you're burning in hell," she yelled, spitting.

Betty boosted herself out of the grave and left it uncovered—dawn was breaking.

Do I risk trying to find one of those bodies, or do I get out of here and live to fight another day? I could give it another hour of searching . . . Maybe find the grave and come back for the body tomorrow night?

Wiping moisture from the bridge of her nose, she was startled when her phone cried out from her rear pocket. It was an alarm she'd meant to set for five o'clock in the evening, but must've had a slip of finger and set it for morning instead. She had forgotten she'd been invited for a night out drinking with a man she'd met online.

She wasn't too happy about it, but hadn't completely

given up on the idea of conceiving a baby the old-fashioned way.

The man she was to meet tonight wasn't her type by any stretch of the definition, but he wasn't the bottom of the barrel from what she could tell, so far. He'd earned points by continuing average conversation without sending an unsolicited dick pic or asking to see her tits. Still, what sort of man would stoop so low as to resort to using the Internet to meet women?

Her train of thought set off her internal hypocrisy alarm. Many things can happen to drive a person to meeting a total stranger off the Internet rather than the natural, olde-worlde way.

With a heavy sigh, she resolved to pack the crypt-kicking in for the day. She'd already agreed to meet and needed to give the guy the benefit of the doubt for at least the modicum of effort on his behalf. If she dug up another coffin before even getting started with the day job, she'd be far too tired to make herself look nice and put up the façade of a professional woman with a desire for human affection.

She rolled her eyes at the thought.

***

Looking in the mirror, Betty smacked her red lips as she leaned over and squeezed her tits together. Given the proper incentives, she could make herself look quite presentable. Perhaps she had overdone it for a first date but had had fun making herself look so sexy nonetheless.

Her phone beside her on the bathroom counter buzzed. Glancing at it, she read:

GLENN
im prkd out frnt

The lack of vowels caused her stomach to turn.

Another sigh escaped her as she grabbed her clutch and made for the front door.

As soon as the cool air wrapped around her shoulders, she almost lamented not heading out to the burial grounds. Going out for drinks seemed so . . . mundane in contrast.

From the driver's seat of the early-model tan Hyundai sedan, Glenn leaned over and shoved the door open for Betty.

What a gentleman.

"You must be Betty," said the man who looked at least ten years older and fifty pounds heavier than his profile had indicated. His eyes bulged behind his chubby cheeks and the breath escaping through his untrustworthy smile sounded thick in his chest. At least he made the effort to look up from her cleavage multiple times as she squatted to enter.

"Not a bad guess. And you must be . . . ?"

Glenn laughed a little too hard and she uncomfortably followed suit. He continued to stare at her from beneath the brim of his fedora as she buckled her seatbelt. As she looked out the windshield, she regretted her stupid choice to give this huge piece of shit the opportunity to sire her child.

"So, where do you wanna go?" he asked, leaning in far too close. His smile hadn't wavered, but the smell emanating from him was much more potent from this distance. "Haha! I'm just messing with you." He clapped a hand on her exposed thigh, causing her skin to crawl. "I already know where we're going. Cheap drinks and good tunes are hard to beat. Am I right or am I right?"

Scrunching her face and pursing her lips to convey something other than disgust, she gave a nod. *Yeah, a bar sounds like a real stretch from your daily routine.*

Looking down, she noted the breathalyzer device connected to his ignition.

Glenn shifted the vehicle into gear and the pair took off down the road.

***

After a drive that left Betty feeling more uneasy than she could recall in recent history, the Hyundai pulled up to a building sided with rough wooden planks and sporting a giant neon sign that flashed Lucky Larry's in glowing purple letters.

"This place is the best," he said, reaching for his door handle.

Betty assumed this gift to womankind wasn't about to come around and open her door—with leaning over her to grab the handle no longer an option—so she let herself out. Upon releasing the lever, she felt a sticky residue cling to her hand. "You come here often, I take it?" She tried not to sound like she was about to throw up, but didn't think he noticed her fail in that endeavor.

"Oh, yeah, I come here *all* the time! Larry and me—we're practically best buds." He smiled from ear to ear.

"Then I'm sure it's an incredible place." This time, her facetious filter failed to engage, spilling sarcasm all over the parking lot. Once more, Glenn was oblivious as he made a beeline for the door. Tailing him slowly, she said under her breath, "If they don't have good fries, you're going to be my next corpse so at least *something* goes my way tonight."

Inside, she found Glenn sitting at the bar already filling another patron's ear full of what Betty could only assume was nonsensical drivel. She looked around at the many empty tables that adorned the restaurant portion of the building, back to Glenn, and to the tables.

One simpleton would be more than enough for the evening, she decided. She tossed her clutch onto the bench of a nearby booth and slid in after it. Thankfully, there was already a menu on the table. She flipped it over to see the appetizers and was delighted when she found something called Clam Chowder Fries. On the other side was the cocktail menu. After a quick glance, she found an Apple Washington and figured she could pound enough of those to make herself have a decent night despite her company.

"Hey, there ya are!" Glenn said, scaring the shit out of her and sliding into the booth across from her. His beer sloshed to and fro, spilling over the sides as he moved.

She snatched up the menu to have something better to look at than the disappointment before her.

"Sorry about that. That's my buddy, Mutt. Ya know, he said he ain't never seen someone as pretty as you. I mean, maybe he didn't say it quite like that"—Glenn smiled, jiggling as he chuckled—"but that's the basic gist of it."

"Charmed, I'm sure," she said, glaring over the menu.

"Oh—my God!" exclaimed the waitress who'd just arrived, notepad and pen in hand. "I *love* your dress! You look so pretty! What are you doing *here*? Glenn, aren't you going to introduce us?"

"Hiya, Toots. Where are my manners? This fine thing is my date for the evening, Betty. Betty, this is Toots."

"My name is Joanna," she said, extending a hand. "Don't believe a word out of this one's mouth." She gave a friendly wink before asking, "Can I bring you something?"

"Yeah, could I get an Apple Washington and the Clam Chowder Fries, please."

"OMG," the young waitress exclaimed in text-speech. "Those are literally to die for."

"Nah, fuck that garbage," Glenn interrupted, wiping the foam from beer off his upper lip. "The fries here suck. We'll get the Macho Nachos! Now there's your headline dish, darlin'." He winked at Joanna before going back to his beer.

"Oh, no. I'd really like to get the fries, please. He doesn't speak for me."

"No problem at all. I'll have that out for you in no time!" Joanna gave a joyful smile and headed toward the bar.

Across the table, Glenn's face soured. "Honestly, the nachos are, like, ten times better than the fries here. You're making a huge mistake."

"You might be right, but I'm going to try to enjoy myself anyway." Negativity and pessimism had ruled much of her life, but never once had she let it break her. Instead, she'd let it guide her in finding ways to enjoy life when it seemed more like an enemy than a friend. A smile, false though it may be, always had the tendency to make her slightly happier than when she wore a scowl.

Sure, she'd been duped into spending the evening with a total troll, but she could drink and hopefully eat something tasty and relish time spent indoors rather than down in a hole in the ground with an infestation finding its way into her panties . . .

But then again . . . . The thought made her grin, and Betty had to swallow a laugh.

"Anyway," Glenn said as he swirled the beer at the bottom of his glass, "what's new with you? You get the chance to knock-up any women today?"

She couldn't help but smirk at the simplicity of the way he described granting the gift of life to a couple that otherwise wouldn't have the ability to conceive. "As a matter of fact, it was a pretty interesting day," she said, thinking of this morning. Glancing down at her hands, she noticed she still had some dirt beneath her fingernails. Nonchalantly, she scraped it out and went on. "I had the chance to aid the most incredible young people I've ever had the pleasure of meeting. He was a young man who designs machinery with the intent of replacing child labor in various harsh conditions around the world. He was inspired by a recent trip to South Afri—"

"I gotta take me a piss," Glenn said, standing and chugging the remainder of his ale.

Betty's eyes went wide as he walked away. Almost inaudibly, she uttered, "Are you fucking kidding me?"

Thankfully, Joanna approached with the drink she'd ordered. "Here you go, sweetie." She turned to head back from whence she came, but Betty grabbed her by the elbow.

"Hang on a sec," she said. "What's the deal with this guy, Glenn? Is there anything . . . *off* with him?"

Joanna smiled and rolled her eyes. "I think he prides himself on his ability to seem normal through the filter of the internet. I'm pretty sure he's harmless, though. He's come in here with an unreasonable number of attractive ladies such as yourself. Some stay and put up with his scatterbrained antics, while others check out on him. Bottom line is, sweetie, you can do whatever's best for you and find no guilt come morning." She patted the back of Betty's hand and gave her a wink. "Now, if you'll excuse me, I've got some Clam Chowder Fries to go back and check on, if you think you'll stick around to give them a whirl."

For the first time that night, an honest smile found its way to Betty's lips. "My curiosity has been piqued. On with the fries!"

"Hell yes, girl! That's what I like to hear!"

"Well, if it isn't my two favorite girls," said Glenn as he slid back into the booth. "Now, should the urge to start making out with each other strike, don't hold back on my account, haha!"

The two women exchanged looks of disgust before Joanna turned her back on them and made her way to the kitchen.

"So, *Toots* was telling me you come here quite often. Typically, with various female companions. Is that so?"

Glenn held up his glass and drank from it—streams of booze fell from the corners of his mouth. "Well," he said, stifling a belch, "I wouldn't say it's all that often I try to meet a nice girl. I have brought a few here. This place is like a second home to me. It's where I feel comfortable and can be myself.

"Look, I . . . I know you probably like the text version of me more, but it's really hard for me to be that much different for very long face to face. To be blunt, I like you. On the internet, I feel like we really connected. I hope, even though you've seen how I'm really like, maybe you'd be willing to see past it and get to know the me you've seen tonight as well as the man you got to know through text. What do you say? Why don't we give it a shot?"

Betty detected sincerity in his eyes. "I think you're vile and grotesque. Regardless of whether or not you're being honest this moment, I think you're a fake piece of garbage who lures in trusting women and wastes their time. Not only will I *not* give this a shot, but I don't even want to enjoy my fries and drink around you. Please get away from me."

Gracefully, she lifted the green beverage from the table and tilted it to her ruby red lips before taking a long, slow pull from it. "Mmm, that's yummy," she said, smacking her chops. Looking up from the drink, she saw tears well up in Glenn's eyes and begin to fall from his eyelashes. "What are you doing, you disgusting piece of trash? Be gone." She shooed him away with the back of her hand. "It's about time a lady cut you down to size, boy."

And so, her decision for the night was made. Most of the men she considered to be decent quality were out of her standards, according to her overdeveloped sense of self-loathing. Men that were attainable by regular means were only slightly better than finding a less advanced species of ape. The dead were available. She only needed to prepare herself better and find a specimen that would yield her a child.

"Careful, they're hot," Joanna said as she slid the plate of fries onto the table. "*Bon appetit*!"

Following the purchase of another beer to take with him, Glenn got up and retreated to a darkened corner of Larry's. By this point, tears were sliding down his cheeks and Joanna was pointing and laughing at him from behind the bar. She was also saying something to him which Betty couldn't make out, and it wasn't until Joanna came over with her third drink that she inquired about it.

Joanna winked and smiled as she sashayed over. "You've ditched your date then, hon?"

"Yes, definitely. He was creeping me out, and he's nothing more than a bushwhacking slob. A troll of the highest magnitude, Joanna. What did you say to him?"

"I was making fun of him for crying and bitchin' like a little sissy-ass girl. I was tempted to hand him a tampon."

Betty laughed and almost choked on her drink. "Oh, dear. Good one!"

"Enjoy the rest of your evening, hon."

When Betty turned to her drink, her eyes drifted to where Glenn sat. From within his poorly lit crook, he glared. Betty could feel his weasel-like eyes all over her body, prompting her to pull the V in her dress together, but she knew it wouldn't stay that way. Still, she continued to enjoy herself and ordered more drinks and food as the night pressed on.

Come nine o'clock, a band took to the stage and she partook in a number of dances with men she considered rednecks, truckers, and beer-chuggers. And, even though such brutes were not her type, it didn't stop Betty from having the time of her life, which was something she'd almost forgotten how to do. She couldn't recall the last time she'd smiled or laughed out loud, even if it was at the expense of someone else—someone *below* her.

It was about time another was the butt of a joke, and after this experience with such a ne'er-do-well as Glenn, Betty was *definitely* done with men.

Well, warm ones, at least.

She smiled and hiccupped.

Once the dizziness set in and slanted her vision, Betty knew it was time to leave.

Another drink, she argued with herself, calling Joanna over. "One for the road, please!"

"You got it, chick."

"Oh, and could you call me a taxi while you're at it, please? I think it would be rude of me to ask Glenn for a ride home!" She laughed hysterically, slapping her thigh and grabbing Joanna by her forearm.

"No *problemo*." After giving Betty a cheeky wink, Joanna set off.

All the while, Betty watched the barmaid strut across the room, admiring how her petite backside swayed beneath her tight, faded blue jeans.

After Betty drained her ninth and final Apple Washington, Joanna called over to inform her that her taxi was outside, meter running.

"Take care, darlin'," Joanna said.

Before Betty made her way out the door, she weaved her way to the bar and placed her card down on it. "If you fancy hooking up for a drink and a chat, give me a call, Jo." Betty slipped her hand over the other woman's and their eyes locked for the briefest of moments. "I best be off." When she pulled her hand away, she winked and zigzagged toward the exit.

Betty turned for a fleeting look, and that's when sobriety blindsided her, stealing her breath.

Where did he go? I thought he was—He's probably in the john, she thought, eyes frantically searching Larry's for Glenn. *Does it matter?*

It does if he's waiting for me outside.

Then she laughed, thinking her 'date' a weak and pathetic fool.

He wouldn't have the balls to try anything.

Outside Larry's, Betty found the car park empty save the taxi. Glenn's car was nowhere in sight.

Betty's smile widened as she got into the back of the cab. Settled, she gave the cabby her address.

***

Laugh at me will you, cunt?! Think you're so fucking clever with your words and chemistry shit, don't you? Glenn thought with fresh tears streaming down his face. "Well, fuck you!" He rattled the steering wheel as he drove, which made his car swerve into oncoming traffic—an eighteen-wheeler blared its horn.

Rain beat against his windshield.

"I should have waited outside for the bitch and given her a piece of my mind. She's lucky to have hooked up with such nice guy. *Pfft*—they're all the fucking same. Whores, the lot of 'em."

A small voice at the back of Glenn's jilted mind spoke; it was firm, friendly, and familiar.

Go back. Go back and tear a strip off her—drive tears from her. See how she likes it. Bitch is fucking ugly anyway.

"Yeah, I should."

Do it, then. We know we have the balls. Look at that bitch two weeks ago we had to . . . correct. *Blackened her eyes but good. Pissed her knickers, too.*

"Huh!" Glenn snicker-cried, his breath hitching in his throat as a snot bubble formed and burst from his left nostril, the mucus spraying the back of his hand.

A turn came up on his right and he took it, getting his car switched around and moving back in the direction he'd come from. Glenn put his foot down, but knew he had no rush—there was plenty of time. Before leaving, he'd seen her dancing with one of the many men in the bar. Also, a fresh drink had been placed on her table. That had been roughly ten to fifteen minutes ago, and he'd only driven a mile or so down the road.

"Gonna tear her a new asshole. Slug her, if I have to. No wiseass bitch is goin' to make fun of Glenn P. Wight!"

Plenty more wool where Betty came from, Glenn— the interweb's full of 'em. Desperate fucks. Like fishing with dynamite.

As he drove, his grip intensified on the wheel, turning his knuckles white.

Within minutes, Larry's came into sight. He turned into the lot. After finding a dark spot beneath overhanging tree branches to conceal his car, Glenn killed the engine and waited. He was willing to stay put for as long as it took.

I've got nowhere to be, unlike her—she has a rendezvous with the Master of Manners. He cracked his knuckles and settled in his seat.

His wait was short-lived, as Betty staggered out of Larry's thirty minutes later.

"Drunk and defenseless . . ."
The taxi pulled away.
Glenn followed at a safe distance.

***

Two things struck Betty in her semi-intoxicated state, as she lay slumped in the back of the taxi. One: she now knew she had a thing for women—well, for Joanna, at any rate. (What she didn't know was whether or not it stretched to women in general.) Two: Betty was horny, and her toy box would need breaking out when she got home—it was unavoidable. If she didn't slake her desire soon, her mind would be a scrambled mess, and she wouldn't be able to get any work done tomorrow.

"Work, work, work!" she babbled.

"You say something, miss?" the driver asked, looking in the rearview mirror.

If I didn't know any better, I'd swear he's looking at my legs . . . "I'm fine, thanks. Maybe you should watch the road?!"

A few minutes later, the cab came to a jerking halt outside her house.

"That'll be fifteen dollars, please, miss. Will you need a hand getting in?"

Bet you'd like to come in for coffee, too. Betty laughed and blushed. "I'm quite capable. Thanks."

The cabby muttered something under his breath as he took her money. After bidding her a goodnight, he pulled off and Betty made her way to her front door. Along the way, she stumbled and dropped her keys.

She laughed like a naughty schoolgirl.

"Where the . . . *Ah-ha*!" After scooping them off the ground, Betty continued on to her beautiful house and crashed against the front door, giggling.

"Good God, Betty! Look at the state of you!" she imagined her mother saying.

Slotting the Yale home, Betty made a raspberry sound and poked her tongue out at her mother. She unlocked the door and started to open it. "You're not the boss of me, Ma. So you can go swivel on my middle—"

A scream caught in Betty's throat as she was shoved hard from behind. She crashed against the door, her grip on the handle lost. As she flew through the opening with her attacker's hands wrapped around her waist, she heard the person yell, as though they'd not expected this to happen.

They must not have realized I'd opened—

Her thoughts were jarred from her when her shoulder smashed against her marble flooring. Betty's teeth snapped together. A front tooth chipped.

"*Ugh!*" the person gasped when they hit the deck with a dense smack.

"*Bastard*!" She pulled her lips back, revealing bloody teeth and gums. Betty wriggled out of the loose grip and crawled toward the spiral staircase. Looking back, she saw her attacker on all fours, shaking their head, which was covered with a balaclava.

Got to get up. Betty scrambled to her knees and made it to the foot of the staircase. *Phone. In my bedroom.* Her breath was slowly returning to her lungs.

Four steps up, and a hand encircled her ankle. This time, Betty did manage to scream. When she looked down, she saw the eyes of her attacker glaring up.

"Fucking bitch! Think you can walk out on *me*?"

"*Glenn*?!"

His teeth were stained red. Blood—she presumed from his forehead—seeped into his right eye. "Gonna teach you a valuable—"

A well-placed heel-kick to his nose crushed the bone, and he released his hold on her as scarlet exploded from his nostrils like ketchup packets being stamped on.

"Argh! *Cunt*!" he squealed like a wounded pig as he reached for his nose. She heard his body roll down the few steps he'd managed to ascend. "Come fucking back here."

His yell vibrated in her ribcage, and her heart missed a beat.

Getting to the top step, Betty could see her phone through her open bedroom door—safety was within reach.

He'll never break through the lock on—

A hand gripped the tail end of her dress, but it felt weak. Betty turned and smashed the heel of her palm into Glenn's obliterated nose.

For a moment, he wobbled on the balls of his feet, teetering before stumbling backward and hitting every other step on his tumble to the bottom.

Sickening sounds of cracking, snapping bones filled her ears, and when he rolled to a crippled, mangled mess at the foot of the stairs, Betty could see splintered ribs poking out of his chest and guts, which reminded her of mini pikes. Gobs of flesh clung to them.

Vomit raced up her throat, but she fought it back down. Tears stung her eyes.

"Glenn? Are you okay? Ambulance?" she asked, knowing how stupid that sounded. *Boy needs a boneyard vehicle, not a meat wagon!* "I didn't mean to kill him! Sweet Jesus."

She descended the stairs, avoiding the splatters of blood in fear she would slip, and made her way to Glenn's mangled body. The closer she got, the more visible his other wounds were: bones protruded from his neck and his left arm was bent at an impossible angle. His open eyes stared at the ceiling.

She put a hand to her mouth, fingers quivering, and thought she was going to cry, but a cackle escaped her. The laugh chilled her, for it wasn't the sound of a sane person.

Have I gone loopy?

Betty swept the question aside. *I have a fresh body for my slab . . . The possibilities are endless. I need to act fast, and not sit here fretting.*

Then another thought hit her: *I might not need my toy box tonight after all!*

After closing and locking her front door, Betty removed Glenn's balaclava to make sure it was *definitely* him before proceeding to drag him toward the cellar and down the stairs. Every time the base of his skull hit a step, it made a sickening thud, until she got to the bottom one, where it made a wet sound.

"Like a mallet pounding meat," she muttered, not stopping to catch her breath.

There was no time to lose. The quicker she could get her serum injected into him, the better her chances of it working.

Not bothering to struggle to get him onto her workbench, Betty rushed to her tools and found the biggest scissors available. She took it over to Glenn and snipped at his pants until they came away from his body with minimal effort; his yellow-stained underwear was also removed.

When Glenn was naked from the waist down, an awful thought struck her: *What if his genitals were damaged in the fall?*

Inspecting them closely with a gloved hand, Betty couldn't detect bruising or surface harm.

I've got to try.

She went back to her worktop and grabbed a needle and small bottle containing a green liquid. It was labeled Scrotal Serum.

With shaking hands, Betty unscrewed the cap, thrust the lengthy needle inside, and drew the fluid up the barrel by pulling the plunger back. With a dosage she felt was adequate, Betty knelt beside Glenn and inserted the metal spike into his ball bag with relish.

Betty marveled as she depressed the plunger and the mystic, jade-colored fluid disappeared into Glenn's body.

Her mouth formed a perfect O as the last bit of serum left the syringe.

Betty removed the needle, got to her feet, and stepped backward, her eyes not leaving Glenn's shrunken pecker, which reminded her of a baby acorn.

Twenty minutes passed.

Twenty-five.

Nothing.

Infantile flames of anger licked at her insides.

Her heart pounded.

Her hands curled into fists, her long nails digging into her palms and drawing blood.

Maybe I didn't use enough?

Maybe his testicles were mashed in the fall?

Maybe he was dead for too long before I got to him?

No, he wasn't dead ten minutes! If it doesn't work after that small amount of time, then it will never work on the de—

"Fucking hell," Betty whispered, seeing a spark of life in Glenn's privates.

At first, she thought she'd imagined it, but there it was again: his dick twitched.

"It's *growing.*"

Betty continued to stare at Glenn's cock, which was now starting to resemble a well-fed slug. As the seconds ticked by, the cock became more engorged. Soon enough, it was solid, and so Betty put her hand to it and slid it down and up the hard-on several times.

She looked at his face to make sure *he* was still dead.

There was no sign of life.

"Going by my calculations, I should get ten minutes of hardness out of him before having to inject more."

Betty rucked her dress up around her waist and pulled her sodden g-string aside. She then lowered herself slowly onto Glenn's stiffness and gasped as it pushed through the folds of her pussy. A lightning bolt of pleasure shot through her guts and a gasp escaped her.

"God, I'm coming."

She grinded against it, hoping it would coax an orgasm from him, and then she wondered if she would know if he'd come or not.

I'm sure I'll feel it.

Betty pushed her fears to one side and basked in the moment, for it tasted of glory and first-time sexual pleasure. Before she knew it, she was in the grip of a third orgasm. She worked her hips harder, faster, her fingers digging into Glenn's cold thighs.

"Oh, *fuck*."

And then she felt his dick shrivel inside her.

"No, no, no!"

She got off him, legs shaking, and saw he had shrunk to nothing.

"Did he . . . ? I wonder. I can't tell. Fuck."

She grabbed the serum, filled the plunger, and injected his balls.

The wait was painful, and all kinds of crazy thoughts washed over her.

Maybe it won't happen a second time.

God, I can't believe it worked at all!

I'm going to be rich and famous, not to mention be a mother!

And then the unthinkable happened: Glenn's fingers moved, and his leg jerked.

"Urgh . . ." he groaned. His head tilted to one side, and the bones there creaked and cracked.

"Impossible. He's dead. Dead!"

But there he was, stirring, moving before her very eyes.

"Gonna rip you a new asshole, bitch," he slurred, attempting to sit up.

Betty looked to her left, then her right, trying to find a weapon to use on him. And then she remembered the needle she was holding.

Get the fucker through the eyeball.

About to rush him, the sight of his growing hard-on stopped her dead, and Betty watched in disbelief as it started spitting come for a number of seconds.

When it stopped, all life drained out of Glenn and he flopped down dead for a second time.

The time for her analytical mind to comb over the whole, partially drunken memory would have to come later. Now, it was time for her to be proactive and collect the sample she had successfully retrieved.

Like a bolt, she took off toward her home office to gather a syringe from a bag of various medical supplies, so she could scoop up the muck from her cellar flags. She zoomed back, sliding to a stop beside the creamy goo on the cold, hard floor. With her face inches from the puddle, she sucked it into the tube, all the while doing her best to remain optimistic.

Once she had her sample, she reached over to the remainder of the mess and touched it with the tips of her fingers. It had lowered so much in temperature that it barely differentiated from the ground itself.

"God fucking dammit!" Her scream reverberated throughout the room. As she sobbed, she folded into the fetal position. She wasn't aware that when her head touched the floor, it landed in the cooled cream. Tears fell from her eyes as snot oozed from her nose, all coming together to form a putrid mix of human discharge. "What the fuck am I going to do now?"

After sobbing for several more seconds, she tried to compose herself. She hadn't given up after her past setbacks and she wouldn't let this failure be any different. She refused to be the victim of the cosmic joke known as life. Given the options of doing what's hard to succeed and be happy in life versus succumbing to weakness and living a joyless life of misery and conformity, there was no choice. A woman with the power of knowing what she was worth could achieve anything she wanted—the only thing holding her back was her own fear.

Betty sat up, wiped away her tears, and sniffed up whatever muck had collected around her nose. She then forced the goop from her throat into her mouth before spitting it onto Glenn's face. "This piece of shit isn't even worth digging a hole for." The barrel of hydrofluoric acid she had stowed away in the corner of the basement would dissolve any physical evidence of his ever having been there.

She cleaned more of the mess from her face and was surprised to find it covered in the disgusting fluid. "Oh, you son of a bitch!" She punched the corpse in its squishy belly and laughed at the amount of force with which the fat repelled her fist. Feeling slightly better, she mopped up the rest of the cold come from her skin. "Come on, fat boy. It's into the barrel with you."

***

After dragging her date across the cold basement floor closer to her workbench, she sat at her desk to rest and try to put the night into perspective. First off, she had forced herself out of her comfort zone by going to meet yet another guy from the internet she'd known wouldn't be worth her effort. Sure, it hadn't worked out in hindsight, but it was the trying that counted. As much as she would have liked to discount the rest of the human race and go strictly for dead dudes, she knew there were decent people out there. It wasn't her fault that they were so few and nothing worth searching for.

But the *real* story of the night was that beautiful stream of jism that had so gloriously erupted from that pathetic excuse for a cock. Finally, her serum had performed as expected. Well, there was the matter of having resurrected a corpse into . . . a messiah? A zombie? A monstrous creation?

A thought briefly fluttered through her mind: *Maybe I should research deeper into stimulating the neural cortex and reanimating dead corpses in place of necrotic semen rejuvenation?* She shook her head. That wasn't what she wanted. It wasn't about the notoriety or the money. It was only about fulfilling her own dreams of becoming a loving parent and finally finding acceptance from her own mom and dad.

No, she would not change her field of study. Instead, this inspired her only to do better. It encouraged her to try new things to get what she needed in life. This freak accident would be the catalyst she needed to finally get her dream accomplished. If not the next attempt, one after that would surely yield the desired outcome!

But, for now, she had the task of chopping Glenn into small, dissolvable bits and cleaning the DNA evidence from the heinous crime scene.

She looked around the large basement. Upon spying the lab coat on the back of her chair, she stood and stripped down to her birthday suit. Her clothes would all have to be burned.

Next, she walked to the table near the bottom of the stairwell to turn on some music: Andante Favori in F Major by Ludwig van Beethoven. She walked back to Glenn, grabbed him by the wrists, and finished dragging him over to her operating table, which was centered in the room. She rested his arms against it, walked around to the other side, and tugged on his wrists, trying to hoist him up. It was a futile endeavor.

She walked back around and shoved him from the bottom. His body was too flimsy to be pushed up with any degree of accuracy. Instead of rising to the table, he drooped back down and landed face-first on the floor like a wilted flower.

"Fuck it, I'll do it on the ground," she said, straddling the dead body, sweat dripping from her forehead and onto his blood-crusted face. "Sure, on the table and in the proper light would have a romantic movie vibe to it, but down here? In this poorly lit space?" She put her nose to his, used her thumbs to pry open his eyelids, and stared directly into his eyes. "This scene can have a beauty of a different nature. I do not require perfection—I only require results!"

She stood, walked around the body, and continued until she reached the cabinet resting against the wall. A smile spread across her face as if the tools within had greeted her with a song. An overhead light shone upon the various surgical equipment, power tools, and assorted knives, reflecting their light back onto Betty's face, brightening it like a star. She felt like a kid in a candy store.

"How do I wish to cut thee? Let me count the ways . . ." She let her hand glide across the various instruments, letting each have its opportunity to speak. The tool whose song she found most appealing was that of the reciprocating saw. She grasped it around its base and removed it from its place. She liked the weight of it in her hand. "Ah, this should make fast work of you," she said, turning to her patient.

Walking back to the corpse, she gave the trigger a quick squeeze to ensure it was properly charged. The mechanical sound exhilarated her. With her left hand, she caressed her naked body, sliding from her hip, up her side, and finally cupping her breast.

A gentle groan escaped her throat as she became more excited.

"If I'm being entirely honest with you, Glenn, I did *not* think I would be naked in the same room as you ever, much less on the night we met. You are everything that is wrong with this world—a stupid, selfish, utterly worthless lump of human flesh. I'm sure you will not be mourned but, thanks to me, you will be remembered. You will live on in infamy as the one who helped me realize that I am through with actively searching for the right man. There just aren't enough good people out there to go around for all of us, unfortunately." She stopped at his side and scanned him from head to toe before stepping over his body and squatting on top of him.

She leaned close, touching her nose to his again. "And, you'll also be remembered as my first murder," she whispered. She slowly sat back up—a menacing cackle rolled up from her belly. "Most importantly, you'll be remembered as my first test subject to perform as I had hoped. I bet that's the first time you've ever received such a compliment. It's almost sad that you're too dead to hear it."

She placed the cold steel blade against his throat and pulled the trigger. The sharp teeth chewed through the soft skin, into his esophagus, and sent tiny chunks of flesh, hair, and blood flying in all directions. It shocked her to feel the spray across her body, though she had anticipated it. Her smile faded, but not due to lack of joy. She licked the blood from her teeth and spat it back into his face as the blade sliced through his spine as if it were a mere candle.

As the saw worked its magic, she relished the vibrations that rippled through the rest of the corpse, stimulating her clit. She gently grinded against the pelvis of the body. A joyful ripple raced through her as the head fell from its stump.

"Does this count as my first one-night stand?" she asked before moving the blade to his shoulder. "Got to be honest with you, fat boy—never thought I'd get head on a first date!"

***

Betty squatted over the carved-up man, driving the saw to the end of its final cut through the torso. As it did, she allowed the base of the tool to buzz against her pussy. She cried out in ecstasy, coming as the sharp steel ripped through the last piece of meat.

She fell backward onto the floor. Staring at the ceiling and caressing her tits, she huffed and puffed, and wiped some of the fresh blood and sweat from her brow with the back of her red-stained hand. "I'll take a trusty power saw over a live man any day of the week." She glanced to the left to find the foot she had haphazardly tossed after removing it just for fun.

"Right. Back to work, then." She gave her nipples a flick and got to her feet. "Safety first." She bent to pick up the saw and walked it over to set it on the center table. As the music reached its crescendo, a feeling of pride cascaded through her. She would get away with murder, no questions asked. She walked to the barrel of acid and, as she pried the lid off, she realized that her first human trial would also go entirely undocumented. As far as the outside world was concerned, Betty was just an average, boring, early-thirties, single female doctor.

The liquid inside smiled back at her as it reflected her image. "What wonderful times we'll have together, gorgeous," she said to the woman in the barrel. In that moment, she felt beautiful. And powerful.

The lid fell from her hand and landed with a loud clang. She walked back to the pile of Glenn. "Give us a dance, why don't you?" she asked as she picked up a foot and calf. With the pieces in hand, she twirled about for a moment before her bare foot found wet blood and slipped out from beneath her. She fell to the floor, smacking her face into the hard flagstones.

"God fucking dammit," she said, sitting up and rubbing near her temple where her skull had struck the floor. She was unable to tell whether or not she was bleeding. She hoped she wouldn't get any of the corpse's treated blood mixed in with her own, so she stopped touching it and continued on with her task, with much less glee than before.

Gently, she lowered piece after piece of Glenn into the acid until all that was left of him was drying to her basement stairs, floor, and her skin.

Before continuing, she sat beside the barrel and rested. She didn't think she had a concussion but felt it necessary to resist the urge to sleep. "Come on, Betty. No one ever got anywhere by sitting on their ass, grumping about. On your feet, missy. We've got shit to do."

She sighed. "If you insist, Betts," she said to her more resilient side. "I'll grab the mop."

***

Round and round the red water swirled as Betty stood beneath the hot spray.

Before Glenn had arrived, she'd assumed she'd be standing in the shower at some time during the night to scald the shame off herself. Now, she stood there with a smile, watching her victim's blood wash away. Never had she been so pleased to have set her work aside to go out on a date.

For a moment, she wondered if this was what love felt like. But what, exactly, was it that she loved about tonight? Certainly it wasn't Glenn, but what if it had been the act of killing him that she had enjoyed so much? Did the urge to murder still lurk somewhere deep within her?

Whatever it was, she would find a way to make the feeling continue.

***

Two weeks later, Betty decided enough time had lapsed: Glenn's remains were now ready for disposing.

She went down to her laboratory, lifted the lid off the barrel with aid of rubber gloves, and peeked inside. Nothing seemed to remain other than a thick, soup-like substance. To make absolutely sure, she took a metal rod from off her workbench and stirred the goop. Tiny bits of bone fragments swirled within the mixture of blood, acid, and body fluids that had a creamy center when whirled. Hair particles clung to the bar Betty used, which she wiped clean with her thumb and forefinger before replacing the matted mess with the rest of the stewed Glenn.

"Perfect!" she exclaimed, looking from the barrel to the drain in the floor.

After replacing the lid, Betty grunted and groaned as she shoved, tugged and pulled the barrel closer to the runoff. When she was mere inches from it, sweating and breathing hard, she again removed the container's lid and tossed it to one side.

Betty then bent and tugged at the drain, successfully removing the grate so none of the bone splinters would get caught in its metal mesh.

"This is going swimmingly, Glenn," she said, looking up at the man's resting place. Betty straightened and grabbed the rim of the barrel. With all her might, she heaved at it—the contents slopped and swished, with some spilling over the side and splashing the floor.

"Come on, come on."

The acid bath crashed over, knocking Betty off-kilter. She struck against one of her many shelving units. Bottles rattled and clattered, and she gasped with anguish when her latest batch of serum smashed to the concrete—it mixed in with Glenn and swished down the drain.

"*No!*"

All she could do was watch as every drop of it disappeared.

Tears came, hot and angry. Betty took the metal rod and swiped more bottles off her shelf, along with books, test tubes, and various receptacles for mixing—none of it mattered anymore. Glass exploded, with tiny fragments jumping at her face and nipping her here and there, but it didn't stop her.

"It took months—*months*—to perfect that serum."

Her rage swelled, and she suddenly felt like the Incredible Hulk.

Betty upended the metal trolley bed for patients—the noise brought a satisfying smile to her face—before going on to club and obliterate everything in her path with the steel implement.

"My work is ruined. *Argh!*"

She threw the rod to one side and pulled at her

clothes and hair until the fire in her died, leaving her spent and giddy.

Betty hit the deck, rolled into a ball, and cried.

***

"Travis? *Travis?!* Where in the hell are ya, boy? Bet you lookin' at 'em there skin magazines again in the dark, ain't ya? Probably stroking one off, too. Goddamn pervert." Randy shined his flashlight up the darkened tunnel, which had lights here and there along the ceiling. Some were dark, the bulbs dead. "We need to get someone down here to fix 'em," he said, adjusting his hardhat. "Travis? Stop muckin' 'round and get over here. Not scared of the ratties, are you?" A goofy, child-like laugh escaped the fifty-something-year-old, who was an unkempt mess.

Randy turned away and pulled the sewer's blueprints from the pocket of his waterproof pants. He unfolded it and shined his light on it. "Okay, says here the problem—"

"Boo, Pa!"

"Holy hell, Travis," Randy said, dropping his flashlight and paperwork. "Damn near gave me a heart attack."

"Ha-ha!"

"I knew getting you this job was a bad idea—all ya do is mess about. If the boss finds out, you'll get canned."

"Now just hold your wad there, old fella. Who's gonna flap? *You?*"

"I just might. Now, pick up 'em damn sewer plans and get hustling. You ain't too old to go over my knee."

"Okay, okay—don't go pissin' your panties over it, old man. I was just foolin' is all."

"Go fool somewhere else. Men don't play games. They work, and we gots to keep food on the table and a roof o'er our and Ma's head."

"Sorry, Pa."

"Just what were you doin' back there?"

"Taking a piss."

Randy shook his head and snatched the flashlight from his son's large mitt. "Go, before I whack you o'er the head with it."

The two men shuffled through the darkness until they stood beneath the drain belonging to the house they'd been called out to investigate.

"You reckon that highfaluting bitch up there in that house has been flushing her jewelry down her head?"

"Hold your tongue, Travis—she's a fine-lookin' gal."

"I never said she wasn't, did I?"

"Then don't be so disrespectful."

"Damn, I was—"

"What's that noise?" Randy interjected, turning his light from the drain beneath Betty's house and shining it at a pile of rats that had gathered in a corner.

"They're huge, Pa. Beastly."

"Biggest damn vermin I've ever seen, and I've been working these sewers twenty years or more."

Both men kept their beams trained on the rats.

"What in the hell they doin'?" Travis stepped closer to inspect and noticed the rats were lapping at pools of liquid with an unusual color to it. They were also fighting over scraps of bone. "That smell!" He pressed his nose against the cuff of his waterproofs.

"Get back from there, Travis! We got work—" Randy stepped forward to grab his son by the shoulder and kicked a stone in the process. It rattled along the floor, skidding into the feeding frenzy and scattering them.

As they scampered, some of the rats turned their heads, revealing toxic-green-colored eyes. Gore dripped from their larger-than-normal maws; their whiskers were stained red.

"*Fuck*!" was all Randy had time to say before the black and red mass engulfed father and son.

The sound of ripping, squawking and squelching ensued.

"Get. The. Fuck. Off!" Travis screamed as he fought his way free, his face a running mess. He clubbed at the rats one at a time, staving in their grossly misshaped heads. Brains spattered his clothes. When he got to his knees, he turned to see if he could help his dad, but Randy was covered. "Pa? Pa?!"

There was no response.

Torn and bloody, Randy staggered from the angry swarm and made his way up the tunnel, unclipping his radio as he went. "Emergency!" he bellowed into the walkie-talkie. His hand shook. "We have a problem down here—send help at once." His breathing came in ragged rips. He looked over his shoulder, eyes darting left to right.

Keep moving, he told himself, using the wall as a brace.

His radio crackled to life. "Travis, is this you messing around? Copy."

He hit the squelch button. "I'm not fucking around, Regan—send help. *Now!* My pa is fucking *dying* down here."

"There's—"

"Send *someone*!" He threw the radio against a wall and continued his stagger. *Got to get to the manhole . . .*

He heard squeaks and scurries from behind.

Block it out. Don't think about it.

Before Travis knew it, the rats were about his feet, scurrying up his pant legs. They chewed at his knees and thighs as they ripped at his underwear to get to his softy, meaty privates. He screamed and hammered his fists against his body, hoping to kill or dislodge the attackers inside his clothes. As he did this, he lurched forward while stamping on the heads of the vermin closest to him.

The harsh squishing sounds that reverberated off the damp walls around him brought a satisfying, if not somewhat insane-looking, smile to his face. A laugh escaped him.

" 'Ave it, you little fuckers!" Travis ignored the pain shooting up his guts from his groin. Blood pumped from multiple wounds, but he refused to collapse and let them swarm him. "You'll have to try harder." He gritted his teeth, shoving his hand down his pants and grabbing a few rats.

He broke necks, threw others aside, and bit heads off.

When he got to beneath the manhole, with light from above shining down, he laughed hysterically.

Rats still clung to him.

"Anyone down there?" came a voice from above.

"Here," Travis coughed and croaked. "*Here*!"

"What seems t—"

"Get me the fuck outta here, dude. Now." He reached a hand up. "Please . . ."

"Okay, okay—don't get your panties in bunches."

Travis fell against the ladder—the rats kept coming, gnawing at him. He felt his body fold, his vision wavering. Black spots danced before him. "I'm . . . dying . . ." he gasped. When he coughed, blood splashed the wall and rungs in front of him.

The fight was burning out of him and he couldn't tell what the man above was saying. However, he could hear his footfalls on the ladder's steel steps.

"Don't—don't come down here . . ." was all Travis could muster as he fell to the floor. When he opened his mouth to scream, a rat scurried in and clamped its teeth down on his tongue.

"What the fuck?!" the man bellowed, killing off the last of the rats. "You okay?" He flashed his light in Travis' face, who appeared to have stopped breathing. "Holy moly." He unclipped his radio from his utility belt and pressed it to his ear. "Dispatch, we have some big problems—*argh*!"

Travis jumped on his co-worker and sank his teeth into the man's throat and bit down. Flesh tore and blood jettisoned, but the wound wasn't fatal.

"Going to *fuck* you!" Travis told his colleague. "Can you feel the hardness in my pants?" As if to press his point home, he thrust his hips. "I'm going to come, come, and come again, and when I'm done with you, I'm going up top to fuck some more."

"Ugh-*argh*!" The man's jowls wobbled as he sobbed. He was helpless to repel the assault. When his knees buckled, he crashed to the floor. His pants and boxers were torn from his body, along with tufts of pubic hair.

And then, his stiffening cock was in Travis' mouth— a blowjob ensued.

"What the—get the fuck—oh, don't stop. Fuck!" the fat, jowly man gasped. Sweat beaded his forehead and dripped off him. "Don't you fucking stop sucking, cunt!" He punched Travis in the head repeatedly with one hand while his free one sought out the zipper on Travis' pants.

The fucking became intense, going beyond anything one could label rough sex. The men started fighting, biting, kicking, scratching, yanking, pulling, sucking, and wrestling, with Travis managing to get on top of his prey. He rammed his dick up the other man's ass.

Travis' hips worked away like a sewing machine until he came. Spent, he rolled off, breathing hard, but he didn't have time to think as his colleague rolled him over and raped him.

Ten minutes later, feeling recharged, both men wanted to fight and kill each other. They foamed at the mouths but decided to set their differences aside when they heard voices close by.

Not giving his colleague the chance, Travis raced to the ladder. When he got to the top, feeling the man below him trying to tug at his leg to rip him back down, he spotted a young couple walking away.

Travis pounced out of the hole and attacked, not noticing or caring that his fat colleague was also on the street, running in the opposite direction toward people he'd spotted.

The night came alive with the sound of screaming and tearing and fucking.

Soon, Travis had a small army of horny men and women at his back, and they were ready to rip the city apart.

***

"What the fuck was that?" Betty said in her bedroom. Sirens wailed in the background as what sounded like a riot played out in the foreground outside.

She scurried over to the window. From there, she looked down at the street to find an enormous amount of activity for two o'clock in the morning. It looked like unrest was happening and she couldn't, for the life of her, figure out why.

She sat on the bed and flipped on the television, finding the local news. There was nothing being reported, so she dialed 9-1-1. The phone hadn't sounded its first ring before she thought better of the situation and canceled the call. The last thing she needed was cops all up in her business, especially with Glenn so recently missing.

She pulled on a large shirt and a pair of clean panties—in the process noticing missed calls from her mother and an unknown number—before rushing back to the window. Car alarms blared and an ambulance sat parked in the middle of the cul-de-sac. Betty couldn't tell if the paramedics had left the vehicle to help someone or if there was already a patient inside it, so her eyes kept darting all around trying to find them.

Several people were fighting, many of whom were stark naked. She spotted her neighbors across the way—a father and son who had recently lost the woman of the house to a tragic car accident—with their pants dropped. The father was plowing his son from behind. This image was simply too much for her to register amid the chaos, so she put it out of sight, out of mind.

In her head, she went through a quick rundown of her present scenario. Two weeks ago, she had accidentally killed Glenn, unexpectedly brought him back to life, managed to extract semen from his living corpse, and watched him die a second time, and, today, she'd gotten rid of the body and other evidence, and lost the last bit of her working serum. Then, as she went to wash the events of the day from her skin, after calling the plumbing service to check her drain for blockage, her neighborhood had decided to lose its goddamn mind.

Her stomach dropped and she felt dizzy as she tried to put it all together. "Oh, fuck . . . Is this something I did?"

Outside, she saw the ambulance rocking. From the rear doors, out fell one of the paramedics. One-legged, she dragged an empty, blood-soaked pant leg behind her. Following the disfigured woman was a man in blue, plastic clothing covered in what looked like mud, with a layer of blood trailing from his face. He wasn't wearing any pants and from his gray bush protruded a massive erection.

Betty glanced back at the father and son who were still going at it in their driveway. The son was caked and it looked like chunks of flesh had been bitten away from his back.

"Boners and carnage everywhere. Holy shit—it's the boning dead!"

She peeled herself from the window. "This is fucking insane," she said as she made her way to the basement. "The police or other authorities are going to intervene— especially with an ambulance already parked out front. They'll come, and they'll ask questions. I've got to do something to help make this go away. Otherwise, there's little to no chance of me coming out of this mess unscathed."

With her mind made up before she even reached the bottom of the steps, she went to her tool cabinet. The chainsaw had never been used, and she had been apprehensive about purchasing it, worrying it was a waste of money. Now, she couldn't have been more pleased with her decision at the time.

She grabbed hold of it, switched it on, and gave the trigger a squeeze to ensure the battery had kept its charge. The beast roared to life and the loud, mechanical sound echoed off the concrete walls. She hummed a song as she pulled and released the button a few times.

"Oh yes, this will do nicely." She smiled as the blade reflected the ceiling light into her eyes.

She charged back upstairs, her bare feet slapping each step along the way. At the top, Betty bolted across the tile floor to the front door and burst through it. The cold night air was there to embrace her, causing her nipples to stand erect. The hairs on the back of her neck pricked as though she were a porcupine.

Like a wide-eyed madman, a chainsaw-wielding Betty stood there in her doorway, squeezing the trigger and deciding which way to go. She hurried down the walkway. Ahead, the spinning lights from the ambulance spilled out onto the black street littered with occasional pools of blood from where the horny fiends had traveled.

The night had quieted. Father and son had vanished. There was no trace of the paramedics.

A huge rat scurried past her, causing her to shriek and whirl around at it with the chainsaw. She managed to catch it just right, sending green ooze and sparks upwards. "Ah, gross," she said, trying to shield herself from the shower of back spray. The gunk smelled of shit and rot as it cascaded down upon her.

She looked at the mess that covered her and was shocked at the color. She hadn't seen it against the black of the street, but it was a darker green than what had been in the tube—likely thickened by the natural blood which had mixed with it. The viscosity of it caused it to slowly run down her skin like thick globs of warm tar.

To her right, a scream broke the silence. Her mind raced. She had no idea how many of the horny fiends there were, but she was under the impression that she would never be able to stop them all and cover this whole thing up. She was far beyond the point of no return, but she'd be damned if she'd stand idly by and let innocent people die as a result of her actions.

Betty grabbed the bottom of her shirt and wiped the filth from her face as best she could. The screaming in the distance continued and she took off toward it.

"Help me!"

The cry came from just ahead. As she ran, gobs of green dripped from the chainsaw blade and plopped onto the street with slapping sounds nearly as loud as her own footfalls.

The flashing lights of the ambulance were now behind her, causing Betty to chase her own shadow. The cries for help continued and Betty shouted out, "Just hold on!" She rounded the rear of a minivan to find a woman on her back trying to defend herself from a naked eleven-year-old boy who had a chunk of flesh missing from his right calf. Betty hoisted her weapon above her head and revved its engine, preparing to bring it down on the vicious kid.

"Not my boy!" The woman wrapped her hands around the naked child, who sank his teeth into her right breast. Betty watched in disgust as the child thrust his hips between his mother's thighs and tore fatty tissue from her chest.

Had the sight been slightly less awful, Betty might have hesitated, but as things stood, she plunged the saw into the back of the boy's skull and kept on pressing down until the woman's body vibrated along to the song of the spinning blade. Chunks of scalp, skull, hair, and the thick green slime spewed forth from the pile. As the tool sank deeper and deeper, the mother's blood also kicked out.

Not until all movement in the boy ceased did she remove the saw. Once she did, the lad fell free, but the mother—with a new hole in her chest—stood from her spot in the driveway and lunged at Betty. Luckily, she was quick with her weapon and managed to decapitate her would-be attacker. The severed head fell, neck-stump down, on her toe. The moist, warm meat embraced the digits of her foot before rolling away. The rest of the corpse tumbled toward her, pushing her back and almost causing her to fall backward as the chainsaw continued to whine.

A glance at the two-story house told Betty there was a possibility of others inside—whether they were alive or had turned into one of these things, she did not know. She decided to go in and check the situation out, following a trail of green slime up the walkway. The front door was open, so she let herself in. Her chainsaw was poised at the ready, her finger tense on the trigger.

Inside, the living room was lit by the blue screen of a TV. It had been mounted on the wall above the fireplace but had fallen to the floor and was spider-webbed from the bottom corner. The rest of the room was in disarray: a couch flipped over, tables shoved askew, lamps knocked down. There was a trail of blood smeared across the hardwood floor. She followed it upstairs.

The steps were littered with pictures that had once hung on the walls. Several of the frames had shattered glass. Using the end of the chainsaw blade, she shoved the bits of glass out of her way so as not to injure herself as she carefully made her way up the stairs. The subtle sound of the blade tapping against the shards was almost deafening in the quiet house.

At the landing, there was a bathroom with its door ripped from the hinges. Inside was a bathtub full of bloody water. Spatter and handprints, both large and small, covered the walls. The bathmat, soaked pink, had been pushed out of the way and wrapped around the toilet. On top of it was a sleeve that had been torn from a paramedic's uniform.

Betty panted as her mind raced and her eyes flicked left and right. Her inspection of the bathroom lasted only seconds before she moved on. She swallowed hard as she made her way toward the room at the end of the hall. A switched-on standing lamp had been knocked over and sat centered in the doorway. The room was painted pink and the curtains had princesses and fairies on them.

She could hear something faint inside the room and approached with caution. She wasn't sure, but it sounded like the occasional slapping of flesh on flesh.

With ease, she peeked inside the room to find the paramedic in the bed, on top of someone else. The man's legs were horribly disfigured as if they had been run over by a vehicle. He was propped up on his arms as he thrust away on the purple bed sheets. Tears welled in Betty's eyes as she imagined the poor, frightened little girl that was likely between the uniformed cripple and the bed. She almost vomited before raising the chainsaw and bringing it down through the midsection of the writhing mass.

She sobbed as green filling poured from the duo. The torso split in two and fell off the bed to reveal not a girl, but maybe the father of the house. Betty began laughing at the realization. Putting down the boy and his mother had been hard, but having to do the same to a sweet innocent girl was something she didn't think she would've been able to follow through on.

Once the spinning blade reached the mattress—jerking it about as it met the springs—she pulled it out and made her way over to the window and parted the curtains. Gore dripped from her face as she looked out at the world. The sun was beginning to rise and she could see smoke billowing somewhere on the horizon. The chaos had spread quickly and she hoped to God that something would be able to contain it.

The quiet outside was deafening now, but she thought she was able to make out the sound of sirens in the distance. *I hope they're heading this way . . .*

Before leaving the room, Betty spied a telephone on the bedside table.

Who would I call? The hospital? I could inform them of what I know . . .

She knew it would be career suicide, but what was she supposed to do? People were dying left, right, and center.

"They're dropping like fucking flies out there!"

Worried her deviant side would overpower her moral standings, Betty picked up the phone but got nothing but silence. The line was dead.

Shit . . . At least when there was a ring—

A noise—the sound of breaking glass—from somewhere inside the house derailed her train of thought.

A cold spot developed in her guts.

She reached for the saw's pull cord, as the tool had cut out, and yanked on it with force.

The chainsaw started but spluttered to a standstill.

"No—shit! Don't do this to me." She tried again, and again, and again, but the saw did nothing. The teeth stayed motionless.

Sweat poured down her face; her cheeks flushed. "Bollocks!" Throwing the tool onto the bed, she scanned the room and found a pair of large scissors lying on a dresser next to some cloth, sewing needles, and a pincushion.

Grabbing the snips, Betty crept toward the door on tiptoes like some sort of cartoon villain and poked her head around the jamb.

There were footfalls on the steps.

The top of a head appeared, followed by hunched, naked shoulder.

"I can smell your dirty, dripping cunt!" He slammed his fist against a wall. "Going to stick my tongue in it and lick your insides clean, girlie-girl. *Mmmm . . .*"

When the tops of his arms appeared, she could see he was heavyset with muscle.

"Oh, no. Now what?" Her voice was a mere whisper.

"I can hear *yoooooou!*" he said in a childlike voice. "Come out, come out, wherever you are."

Betty pulled from the door and looked around the room, spotting the large wardrobe.

It's worth a try.

Slinking to the piece of bedroom furniture, she opened it and got in, clicking the door closed behind her.

Betty held her breath and gripped the scissors tight, her knuckles turning white, as his slow, thumping footfalls crossed the landing.

"I know where you are, little Gingerbread Woman. You can't hide. You can't run."

Betty wanted to scream—to piss—but held herself together and clenched her ass cheeks in case a fart escaped her and created a sound likened to gunfire.

He can't possibly smell *me! Unless their senses have been heightened? It's possible. God knows what dangerous levels of my serum could do to an individual.*

What have I done?

The bedroom door creaked.

A floorboard groaned beneath a heavy load.

Betty hoped her whimpering and thunderous heartbeats couldn't be heard beyond her ears.

A shadow fell across her feet, thanks to the crack between the wardrobe's door and base. The light flittering in through the keyhole was blocked.

Her lips trembled.

Her knees knocked.

When a slight rapping came at the wood, she was powerless to stop the urine from trickling down her leg.

"Little pig, little pig, come out, come out, or I shall be forced to blow your house in!"

Her piss splashed against the wood.

"What's that? Not by the hair on your chinny-chin-chin? Or do you mean on your puss—well, what do we have here? Have you soaked yourself?"

"*Ugh*," she sniveled.

"You're making daddy horny. I love watching a woman piss—"

"*Argh*!" Betty screamed, palming the door open and jamming the scissors into the man's neck. Before she could twist and retract, sending his blood squirting, he punched her so hard in the jaw that she thought she was going to black out, but managed to stay conscious.

On the floor, Betty crawled for the door.

"Help!" she wheezed.

Behind her, she heard a stumble and a crash. She looked over her shoulder. Her tall, broad, muscular attacker had collapsed against a dresser and gone to ground.

Blood pooled at his wound and his face grew ashen.

"Die!" she bellowed, continuing to crawl, knowing he was spent.

"Uch-*urgh!*" he gargled, trying to get to his feet. His knees buckled and he smashed onto the bed. He hit the mattress with such force, it flipped him off and into the air. The man crash-landed onto the nightstand, crushing the lamp and obliterating the phone. "*Argh!*" he roared, arching like a humpbacked bridge.

As Betty crossed the threshold, she glanced back once more. The man had stopped moving.

Ten minutes later, she was on her feet and rushing downstairs. Betty pulled a butcher knife from the wooden block on the granite kitchen top. She also took a cleaver and tucked both weapons down the rear of her pants waistband.

The streets were suddenly teeming with the dead and horny.

Never thought I'd see so many hard dicks and stiff nipples in one place at one time, she thought. "And I've watched a lot of porn," she muttered, scanning the thrusting hips and pumping asses. "I should have stayed in my house, locked the doors and waited for help to arrive, not come out here playing Stallone."

Yes, but we only thought a few of them had succumbed, not the whole fucking neighborhood, a voice at the back of her mind argued.

Scampering across the lawn, Betty picked up a

trashcan lid and a random garden gnome wearing yellow galoshes and holding a fishing rod.

A psycho with rapey eyes jumped at her from the shadows.

Betty slammed the metal lid into the short man's throat, crumpling his windpipe.

She didn't bother finishing him off. Instead, she fled closer to her home—the front door mere feet away and ajar. A welcoming glow peeked around the jamb and splashed across her driveway. She could hear a helicopter overhead, nearby. After a glance up, she saw it had its spotlight on, searching the area.

Make it!

A little girl came at her with a flick knife, slashing at her tits.

Betty blocked the blow with the lid and staved the youngster's head in with the gnome. Bits of brightly colored china exploded into the air like gay confetti.

"Out of the fucking way!" she yelled at a naked old woman blocking her path. As she charged through her, she used the metal disc as a bulbar, crumpling it beyond use. When the ancient hag went down, Betty thought she was home and dry, but the granny grabbed her ankle, anchoring her.

Such strength! Betty went for the cleaver and brought it down on the mature woman's shoulder. Her saggy tits jounced from the sudden impact.

"Get off, bitch!" Betty lashed out with her free foot, her toes connecting with the oldie's false teeth, which popped out of her head and slid along the gravel.

"Ugh!" The grip released, allowing Betty to move, but she was blindsided by two men who reeked of shit, piss, and stale meat. Their erections pressed against her thighs.

"Kill the fucking pig cunt!" the old woman screamed.

Blood pissed out of her mouth and busted shoulder.

The men carried Betty off, each grabbing an arm. By now a third and fourth had joined in.

"Hold her down while I get her clothes off," one of them said.

"Get 'em titties out," another said, chuckling.

"Take your fucking hands off me, ghouls!" Betty demanded. "Fucking redneck hicks!"

"Talk dirty some more, whore," a third said.

Cloth ripped.

Betty felt coolness on her pussy. She gasped.

"No!" She wriggled, trying to kick her legs and flail her arms. They now had her pinned to the floor.

"Hey, stuff this here in her," the giggler said.

Betty felt something claw at her privates. "Argh! What the hell is—*argh*!" Her lungs burned. Tears streamed from her eyes. She felt something enter her—it wriggled inside her guts—and then there was a cock shoved in her.

Hot come spurted.

Then another dick was rammed into her, followed by a third and fourth.

She slipped closer to unconsciousness, her body relaxing.

"Bastards," was all she managed before hearing a voice bellow from the helicopter, its light shining upon her.

Two days later, Betty awoke in a hospital.

The nurse told her that the police had come and rescued Betty and chased her attackers away.

"The situation is under control?" Betty asked.

"Yes, although nobody knows for sure what happened. One of life's little mysteries, I guess. I'm sure some egghead somewhere in the world will figure it out one day."

Betty pulled the sheets to her chin. "Yes," she muttered.

"Now, you get some rest. You should be free to go home tomorrow."

"Thanks, nurse."

"That's quite all right. Anything else before I go?"

"Er . . . yes, as it happens. When the doctors checked me over, was everything . . . okay?"

The nurse's smile was grave. "There was a fair bit of tearing and bleeding, but nothing they couldn't fix."

"And no damage to—" She stopped herself and shook her head. "Thanks, nurse."

"You're welcome."

As promised, the next day Betty was discharged.

When she got home, she decided to give it some time before going back to her research.

Three weeks later, while cleaning, tidying, and organizing her lab in readiness to begin working once again, a sharp pain twisted her guts and she doubled over, clutching the area.

"What in the—*argh*?!"

Betty stumbled to her operating table before falling onto it. She writhed and tore her shirt open. Her eyes bulged upon seeing movement beneath her stomach— her flesh tore, and blood started pouring from her skin.

"*Ugh*!" Her eyes flicked, her gaze settling on a scalpel close by. "W-w—what's in me . . . ?"

Her guts, pussy, and asshole burst open, erupting into a sea of black mini rats, which washed over her like a tidal wave.

When she opened her mouth to scream, the tiny vermin filled the void and nibbled at her tongue and cheeks. Others clawed her face and tore at her eyeballs.

Once there was nothing left of Betty to pick from, the

inky mass gathered on the floor and scurried upstairs and out of the house in search of more food.

Other HellBound Books Titles
Available at: www.hellboundbookspublishing.com

Puckered

Percy is kinky.
Percy is perverted.
Percy is a loner.
Percy is sneaky…

…But most of all, Percy wants to be left alone.

Whether it be a nagging mother or something from his past, it feels like he is always trying to escape something.
Will he be able to find his own peace, or will the real world catch up to him?
There will be blood.
There will be s**t.
There will be unusual sexual kinks.
But most of all, there will be murder…

**Psychological Breakdown
By
David Owain Hughes**

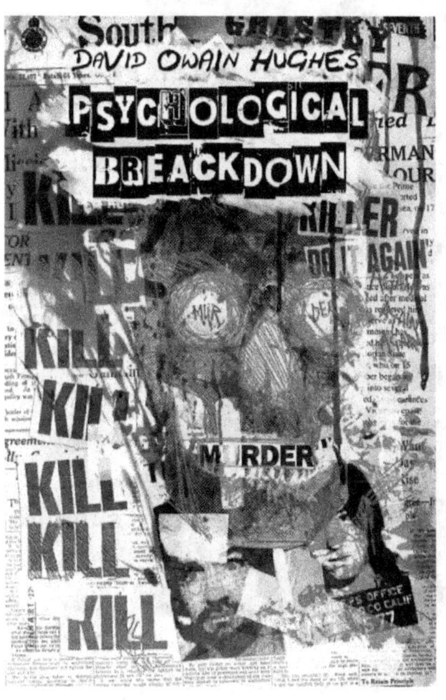

Within this tome lies eighteen tales of mind-bending terror, as Hughes delves into the human psyche and dishes out stories of what becomes of the broken minded, spirited and downright irked.

Part these blood-drenched pages at your own peril, for you will find diseased minds geared towards revenge and bloody chaos, with a few twists, turns and surprises thrown in for good, fucked-up measures.

Keep the lights on!

Man Eating F*cks

A dark, incredibly entertaining excursion into the delightfully twisted imagination of David Owain Hughes....

An average teenage girl and her father find themselves caught up in a brutal nightmare at their local recreational centre, when an age-old enemy comes stumbling out of the woods to crash a heavy-metal gig; a gig that has all the promises of being killer. This is one blood-soaked gig you won't want to miss!

Praise for Man-Eating F*cks from Ty Schwamberger (author of The Fields, Deep Dark Woods & The Death of a Horror Writer.)   "Man Eating F*cks is old school horror, but with a new, blood-soaked twist! David Owain Hughes effectively creates enjoyable and lethal characters in this tale that is sure to keep you up at night. This is the type of tale that you need to read with a light on…I'm serious. You better put your seatbelt on 'cause you're in for one helluva ride. Look out, Hughes might very well be headed to the major leagues after this twisted tale! Highly recommended!"

<u>**Man Eating F**kers**</u>

The eagerly awaited sequel to Hughes' critically acclaimed *Man Eating Fks*...**

Two years on from her nightmarish descent into the woods, Storm is piecing her life back together, but trouble is forming...

A new threat is rising - one that promises to grip, shake and spin Storm's world out of control. But that's not all, as a 'friend' and sympathizer also poses a risk from the shadows, combined with a face from the past...

With the cannibals lurking in the background, waiting for an opportunity to deal white-hot vengeance, can father and daughter survive?

**** Features a bonus, previously unpublished short story by David Owain Hughes****

The Amnesia Girl

Filled with copious amounts of black humor, Gerri R. Gray's first published novel is an offbeat adventure story that could be described as One Flew over the Cuckoo's Nest meets Thelma and Louise.

Flashback to 1974. Farika is a lovely young woman who wakes up one day to find herself a patient in a bizarre New York City psychiatric asylum. She has no idea who she is, and possesses no memories of where she came from, nor how she got there.

Fearing for her life after being attacked by a berserk girl with over one hundred personalities and a vicious nurse with sadistic intentions, the frightened amnesiac teams up with an audacious lesbian with a comically unbalanced mind, and together they attempt a daring escape.

But little do they know that a long strange journey into an even more insane world filled with a multitude of perilous predicaments and off-kilter individuals are waiting for them on the outside. Farika's weird reality crumbles when she finally discovers who, and what, she really is!

Demons, Devils and Denizens of Hell: Vol, 2

The second volume in HellBound Books' outstanding horror anthology fair teems with tales of Hades' finest citizens – both resident and vacationing in our earthly realm…

Compiled by the inimitable P. Mattern and featuring:

Savannah Morgan, Andrew MacKay, Jaap Boekestein, James H Longmore, Stephanie Kelley, Ryan Woods, James Nichols, P. Mattern, Marcus Mattern, Gerri R Gray, and legion more…

Shopping List 2: Another Horror Anthology

Once again, HellBound Books brings you an outstanding collection of horror, dark, slippery things, and supernatural terror - all from the very best up and coming minds in the genre.

We have given each and every one of our authors the opportunity to have their shopping lists read by you, the most wonderful reading public, and have the darkest corners of their creative psyche laid bare for all to see...

In all, 21 stories to chill the soul, tingle the spine and keep you awake in the cold, murky hours of the night from: Erin Lee, The Truth Artist, John Barackman, Serena Daniels, M.R. Wallace, Isobel Blackthorn, Alex Laybourne, Jason J. Nugent, Josh Darling, Jovan Jones, Nick Swain, Douglas Ford, Craig Bullock, Craig Bullock, Jeff C. Stevenson, PC3, David F Gray, Sergio Palumbo, Donna Maria McCarthy, David Clark & Megan E. Morales

David Owain Hughes & Peter Oliver Wonder

**A HellBound Books LLC
Publication**

http://www.hellboundbookspublishing.com

Printed in the United States of America

www.ingramcontent.com/pod-product-compliance
Lightning Source LLC
Chambersburg PA
CBHW071840190726
48292CB00005B/1846